MEL BAY PRESENTS
STRING BAND CLASSICS
MANDOLIN
TRANSCRIBED BY DIX BRUCE

CD Contents

1. Dance All Night [3:16]
2. You Ain't Talkin' to Me [3:34]
3. Money Musk [2:48]
4. There's More Pretty Girls Than One [3:02]
5. Fire on the Mountain [2:18]
6. Gypsy Girl [2:40]
7. Pig Ankle Rag [3:24]
8. Wild Bill Jones [3:45]
9. Sleeping Lulu [3:21]
10. Meeting in the Air [3:42]
11. Hawks and Eagles [2:48]
12. Who Broke the Lock [2:52]
13. Way Out There [4:15]
14. Carroll County Blues [2:30]
15. Old Jimmy Sutton [2:23]
16. Devilish Mary [2:59]
17. Way Down the Old Plank Road [3:15]
18. Tater Patch [2:36]
19. My Dixie Darling [2:47]
20. Free Little Bird [3:11]
21. Been All Around This World [3:25]
22. Goodbye Miss Liza [3:00]
23. Lee Highway Blues [3:41]

Produced Under License from Rounder Records Corp., One Camp Street, Cambridge, Massachusetts 02140 U.S.A.

1 2 3 4 5 6 7 8 9 0

© 2005 BY MEL BAY PUBLICATIONS, INC., PACIFIC, MO 63069.
ALL RIGHTS RESERVED. INTERNATIONAL COPYRIGHT SECURED. B.M.I. MADE AND PRINTED IN U.S.A.
No part of this publication may be reproduced in whole or in part, or stored in a retrieval system, or transmitted in any form
or by any means, electronic, mechanical, photocopy, recording, or otherwise, without written permission of the publisher.

Visit us on the Web at www.melbay.com — E-mail us at email@melbay.com

Contents

Dance All Night 10

You Ain't Talkin' to Me 14

Money Musk 18

There's More Pretty Girls Than One 20

Fire on the Mountain 24

Gypsy Girl 26

Pig Ankle Rag 30

Wild Bill Jones 34

Sleeping Lulu 38

Meeting in the Air 40

Hawks and Eagles 46

Who Broke the Lock 50

Way Out There 52

Carroll County Blues 56

Old Jimmy Sutton 60

Devilish Mary 62

Way Down the Old Plank Road 64

Tater Patch 68

My Dixie Darling 70

Free Little Bird 74

Been All Around This World 76

Goodbye Miss Liza Jane 78

Lee Highway Blues 82

Notes for Highwoods:
by Dix Bruce

Musicians from the Highwoods band studied original recordings from the 1920s and 1930s and sought out surviving musicians from the era to learn about and document the work of these cultural pioneers. Importantly, their primary goal was not to academically copy the music note for note but rather they sought to incorporate the energy, life, humor, and joy of these original old time musicians into their own music. Their success on record and in live performance brought the music to new generations of younger, urban listeners as a vital and living tradition rather than an artifact of a bygone era.

The Highwoods are a great example of youthful and reverent musicians discovering, in the late 1960s and early 1970s, gold in cultures past. With their curiosity, musical talent, and discerning taste, they made the music fun for themselves and their audiences.

My job was to transcribe the melodies, lyrics, chords, and some of the solos on these recordings and prepare versions playable on the mandolin. Since most of the instrumental melodies were played on fiddle, it was necessary to adapt them to mandolin and to the typical ways mandolin is played in this genre of music. I tried to represent melodies as closely as possible and still have them be readable and playable. Some aspects of the performances have been simplified for just that reason. In some cases slight alterations were necessary to make, say, a banjo passage playable on the mandolin.

Generally, I transcribed the first melody heard on the recording. However, if the second or third time through seemed to define more of the essence of the tune as it progressed, I transcribed that. Since most of the fiddle parts are played by two different people (Walt Koken and Bob Potts) on two different fiddles at the same time, the unison melodies are often not identical. This type of ensemble approach encourages artistic license and is very typical of the old time style. You might have three or more lead instruments blasting away at similar melodies throughout the tune. This is very different from a modern country, bluegrass, or even western swing approach where the instruments would act more as a section in a big band or symphony orchestra and play in tight unison or harmony or feature the playing of only one instrument at a time. So, I tried to transcribe what I thought was the dominant melody. In many cases I also included interesting variations the band played on subsequent repetitions of the tune. Of course one can't totally capture on the page all that's being played and sung on the CD. We just don't have the notation technology and it's impossible to communicate all the subtleties of old-time music fully with spots and stems. You gotta listen and after you listen you gotta play it and sing it!

You will notice that several of the selections, while played relatively in tune, are not tuned to standard A=440. To play along with these, you'll need to retune your instrument either sharp or flat depending on the individual song or use some kind of pitch control on your playback machine. It's not unusual to find recorded music that's not tuned to the standard A=440. There can be a variety of reasons for this. Musicians sometimes tune their instruments up to one half step sharp claiming the result is a "brighter" sound on recordings. Sometimes producers speed up master tapes to achieve the same end. Most likely though, the musicians simply tuned to each other and the result was a certain percentage away from the standard 440 A.

Take care when raising the pitch of your instrument. Higher pitches add a great deal of stress to the instrument and if yours is delicate or you push it too far, your ax may fold up like a potato(e) chip. A better solution is to use a tape or CD player with a pitch control, as I did. I was easily able to bring the nonstandard tunings up or down to the written versions.

Most melodies or fragments of melodies can be played at more than one location on the fretboard. For example, one could play a riff near the bottom of the neck and use open strings, or one could play the same thing further up the neck using all fretted notes. For the most part I've written the tablature to these tunes in the lower regions of the neck, unless I heard something specific in the recording that demanded a higher neck the lower regions of the neck, unless I heard something specific in the recording that demanded a higher neck position. I concentrated on the lower positions because I think they are both easier to read and play, and more accurately reflect the way such melodies are played in a typical old time situation.

The small numbers between the notation and tablature staves indicate suggested fretting hand fingers to use to play the notes. In the case of double stops, the upper number applies to the higher note, the lower number to the lower note. I tried to keep these to a minimum to avoid jumbling up the music too much. Most fingerings should be obvious and you should feel free to develop your own. "h" = hammer on, "p" = pull off, "s" = slide, "b" = string bend. If there are several identical notations in a row in the music, I only noted the first one or two. Measure numbers are indicated in the music once per staff above the left hand measure. Measure numbers are referred to in the text in this way: "M 4" = measure four.

Some of the following arrangements include variations that the band played after the initial statement of the melody. These are cases where I found the variation to be particularly interesting. The nature of improvisation in this old timey style is to restate the melody and vary it only slightly upon repetition. The trick is to slip in a few new ideas here and there without losing the feel of the original melody. The Highwoods String Band does this beautifully and it's worth studying just how they go about it.

Below you'll find specific notes on each of the selections. To avoid repetition, some of the intros are quite short as comments from a tune earlier in the book may apply to those later in the book. I'm always tempted to write "This is another great tune you should learn" ... because they are all interesting and worth knowing, so with great effort I'm curbing my typing fingers!

You may find, as I did, that some of these selections are very unusual. Some were difficult to transcribe. But as I discovered their peculiarities, those peculiarities fast became character traits and I ended up loving these challenging songs.

Extra special thanks are due to Laura Alber, Robert Bergman, Steve Powell, and Charlotte Gibb for their most helpful suggestions and assistance in preparing this book. They have the eyes of eagles!

So, read along and play along and have a great time with a wonderful old time band. You can write to me c/o MUSIX, PO Box 231005, Pleasant Hill, CA 94523 or e-mail: dix@musixnow.com. Visit me online at www.musixnow.com. We have a special section where you can download music, TAB, and MP3s of all types of music.

Dix Bruce
April 2005

Notes on the tunes:

1. Dance All Night is a wonderfully energetic three-part fiddle tune with lyrics. The tricky part is the form which, once you listen to it or see it written out, will make more sense. The parts are all labeled in the music but you'll have to a jump around a bit to play along with the recording. Here's the form diagrammed: A-vocal-B-A-A-C-B, A-vocal-B-A-A-C-B, A-vocal-B-A-A-C-B, A-vocal (repeat verse 1)-B-A-ending. The first two bars make up the familiar fiddle double stop introduction. This is done to show the other musicians at what tempo the song will be played. It makes for an interesting effect on other instruments as well. Starting in M 45 I've included a variation on the A part. Feel free to substitute it for the first A part. Beginning in M 53 there are several measures with quarter notes. You'll find this to be quite a switch from the constant eighth notes but it does make for a striking contrast in a solo. (page 10)

2. You Ain't Talkin' to Me has both a verse and a chorus. Unusually, the fiddle introduction, on which the first 32 measures of the transcription is based, is played over both parts. After each vocal verse and chorus, a solo almost identical to the intro is played over the whole form. This song is a favorite of mine because of its hilarious take on the human condition. And, the self serving attitude of the singer is presented without a shred of self consciousness or shame. You can also hear Charlie Poole, one of the most important original sources for old time music, sing "You Ain't Talkin' to Me" on the "Old-Time Songs" (County CO-CD-3501), one of three Poole CDs on the label. (page 14)

3. Money Musk is a straight forward four-part fiddle tune with a good bit of Irish seasoning. I've named the parts with letters, which are boxed, instead of numerals, and the parts are played consecutively. The triplets in the pickup, M 18, 22, 26, 30, 31, may be a challenge for you. M 38 is somewhat unusual with its different melody. You'd expect a repeat of M 34 here but the Highwoods play it a little differently. Try playing a G chord instead of the D. (page 18)

4. There's More Pretty Girls Than One is a beautiful and popular waltz that's kind of a "standard" — musicians all over the world play it — of bluegrass, old time, and country music. Compare this version with Ricky Skaggs and Tony Rice's great 4/4 version on "Skaggs & Rice" (Sugar Hill Records). I suggest you use tremolo on all notes longer than quarters. The introduction has lots of very fiddle-esque double stops. If I was playing this intro on the mandolin, I might shift these around a bit to reflect more of the melody heard in the solo beginning in M 52. Still, there are some very interesting passages that are worth exploring on the mandolin. M 13 of the intro has a triplet figure and in M 16 you'll find another very fiddle-esque lick that we'll play using a hammer on/pull-off combination on the third string while the second string rings. The solo in M 52 will get you working up the neck and give your third and fourth fretting hand fingers some good exercise. The fourth finger D on the first string tenth fret will require some work and you may be unfamiliar with the second and third string notes that follow. Try playing this whole solo tremolo. (page 20)

5. Fire on the Mountain is an absolute "must-know" song. It's a popular, hot and fast rip snorter. As with every tune, take it slow at first and build up your speed as you learn it. Learning it won't be too challenging since the melody is basically four measures repeated again and again in two different keys. Learn the first four bars of the tune and you will pretty much have it licked. "Fire on the Mountain" changes from the key of A to the key D in M 10 and then back again to the key of A in M 18 for a quick two measure tag. The form of the recorded performance holds to the printed arrangement, M 1-19, except after the brief vocal. Here the band returns to the beginning of the tune but doesn't play the repeat of the key of A melody before it goes on to the key of D part and the A tag. After that, the band repeats the tune as written in M 1-19. As I mentioned, the melody is quite simple and repetitive. That probably accounts for its popularity.

The structure of the melody allows for lots of simple variations that don't interrupt the flow or basic shape of the melody. I transcribed some of the band's melodic variations at M 32. Be sure to try making up your own. If you're playing along with the recording, you'll find that the band is almost 1/2 step sharp from standard A=440. (page 24)

6. Gypsy Girl. Be aware of the form on "Gypsy Girl" as it changes with the different lengths of the vocal strains. Strains one and four are 16 measures in length, two and three are 24 measures. Other than that, the arrangement is straight forward: instrumental, vocal, instrumental, etc. Charlie Poole recorded this song as "My Gypsy Girl." (page 26)

7. Pig Ankle Rag is a delightful and underperformed tune with a great raggy feel. I transcribed four distinct parts but you'll hear much variation on melodic passages, especially over the E7 to A7 chord changes, as the parts repeat in seemingly random order. I transcribed the B part as B.1 and B.2 to show several interesting variations on the repeat. Part D is really just part B played an octave higher with some nice variations. I just love this tune, but especially like the slide in M 4 and the double stops in part C. If the double stops give you trouble, try playing only the upper notes. The fretting finger numbers are suggestions only. Feel free to work out fingerings of your own. (page 30)

8. Wild Bill Jones is a classic outlaw/murder song in the tradition of "Jesse James," "John Hardy," and "Staggerlee." I've done something a bit unusual with the transcription. I included two different fiddle solos and showed how they "tagged" the vocal to begin the solo. (M 50, M 69) M 50 and 51 are repeats of M 48 & 49 and overlap the end of the vocal line. It's a little confusing because the measures at those two points are not continuous but I wanted to show how the fiddlers move from the vocal to their respective solos. (page 34)

9. Sleeping Lulu is a bright and energetic fiddle tune with I-VI-II-V ("one-six-two-five") changes (M 16-18) like you find in old time rags. I've put these changes in parenthesis because they aren't played every time. Sometimes they are only alluded to by a guitar bass run. Try playing the tune with and without the extra changes. (page 38)

10. Meeting in the Air. In this transcription I've preserved a lot of the feel of the fiddle parts with longer notes and double stops. I suggest that you tremolo all notes longer than eighths. The two solos, M 82 and 115, are more good examples of how subtly old time musicians change a basic melody upon repetition. Compare both of these solos with the introduction. (page 40)

11. Hawks and Eagles. I transcribed this two-part fiddle tune along with a few variations. Part 2 is quite similar to part 1 except that it's pitched an octave lower. Notice how similar the variations are to the initial statement of the melody. (page 46)

12. Who Broke the Lock is simply great fun! The B chords in parenthesis are more implied than played. I haven't a clue as to whom "Old Bruno," mentioned in verse one, might be. Other versions of the song mention hearing a chicken sneeze. Steve Powell, a mandolinist friend of mine, told me he had to play this one "over and over, for at least an hour" for his five-year-old. Beware, if you play this one for kids, they'll love it! (page 50)

13. Way Out There is another very popular old time and western song. M 24 & 25 overlap. M 24 shows the end of the solo, M 25 shows the pickup to the verse. If you solo over the chorus, use tremolo on the tied whole notes. (page 52)

14. Carroll County Blues. Compare this version with Doc Watson's in my book "Doc Watson and Clarence Ashley 1960-1962" (Mel Bay MB 97056). The introduction to the Highwoods' rendition is played on guitar using a bluesy technique with bent strings. We'll play those passages with a two note hammer combination on the mandolin. The pickup measure to the melody (M 5) overlaps the last measure of the guitar intro (M 4).

The melody that begins in M 5 was transcribed from the second fiddle solo with a few elements from the first solo. This second solo is more typical of the way the melody is played throughout the rest of the recording. I've also included a variation for part 1 beginning at M 40. As you're playing the introduction and proceeding to the melody, you should leave out either M 4 or 5. (page 56)

15. Old Jimmy Sutton is a great example of what I love about old time music. This song is so odd, so out there that you can't help but like it! The concept of the cow as empathetic when he says to the sheep "I did not know" is beautiful! The first part is a combination of unaccompanied vocal and a nine measure fiddle melody that's played at a relatively slow tempo broken up with stops, holds, and "baahs." The second part is played at a breakdown tempo, more in the tonality of the key of A than the key of D. (page 60)

16. Devilish Mary is another funny song with a devilish matrimonial theme. You can use the introduction as a solo. The first lyrics of the chorus are difficult to discern. I hear "Ring come a ding come tarry." Other versions have "Along come a-dink come a-dary," "Along come-a-ding-come-a-daree," and "It's tararinktum, tararinktum, Tararinktum ready!"(page 62)

17. Way Down the Old Plank Road starts out with an unaccompanied banjo solo which I've adapted for the mandolin. After the banjo solo comes a short, eight-measure fiddle intro followed by the vocal. After that you'll find a full twenty four-measure solo based on the full fiddle solo. The Highwoods alternate this with the fiddle intro after each vocal verse and chorus. (page 64)

18. Tater Patch is a straight forward two-part fiddle tune with some interesting and unusual chords and harmony. I've written out two versions of part 1 so you can study two slightly different melodies. (page 68)

19. My Dixie Darling is a song I first heard on a Carter Family recording. The Highwoods' version is beautifully done both instrumentally and vocally and the intro will give you opportunities to play hammer/pull triplets and double stops. Triplets are pretty easy on a fiddle since the bow keeps the sound going. On mandolin, it's more difficult to sustain the sound over three notes played with one pick stroke. One alternative to the triplets is to play only the first note of the triplet as a quarter note. One could also play the first two notes as two eighth notes.

The solo at M 73 is based on one of the few guitar solos on the recording. Try playing it both with and without tremolo. The double stops in M 22, 29, 31, etc., may be a challenge for you, especially if you're not used to playing up the neck. The good news is that once you understand the concept, you'll find double stops and positions up the neck easily adaptable to other positions and keys. Double stops and playing up the neck are important skills for the old time, bluegrass, country, and folk mandolinist to understand and master. Notice the meter changes in M 20, 23, 25, etc. (page 70)

20. Free Little Bird. On the recording "Free Little Bird" is pitched closer to A than to G. I chose to transcribe it to in the key of G but it might be played out of the key of A. Compare this version with Doc Watson & Clarence Ashley's from "Doc Watson and Clarence Ashley 1960-1962" (Mel Bay MB 97056). (page 76)

21. Been All Around This World. In M 10 and 11 you'll find two sets of triplets. Play the first with a hammer / pull combination. Play the second with two consecutive hammers. The late Joe Val recorded a nice bluegrass version of this song on the Rounder CD "Rounder Old Time." (page 78)

22. Goodbye Miss Liza. As I've mentioned, old-time string band music really stresses the melody, as we hear in this selection, with intro and solo being played almost identically. Notice the wonderful ensemble work which demonstrates how this type of music is by nature very democratic. Some might say anarchistic. (page 80)

23. Lee Highway Blues. We round out the set with another of the greatest hits of old time music and one you should know. This version has four parts. The first three are fairly typical fiddle tune-esque melodies but the fourth is a more abstract extended note melody where you'll certainly want to use tremolo. Be sure to check out the Watson/Ashley version. (page 84)

Dance All Night

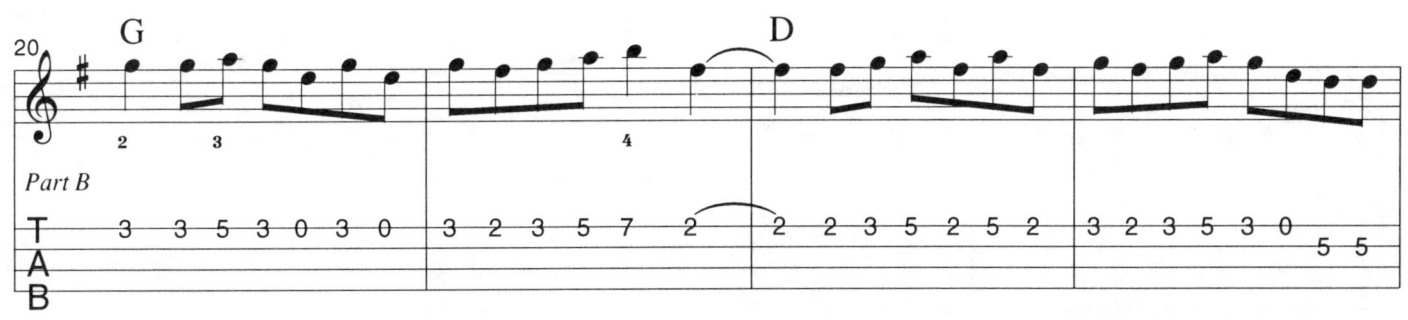
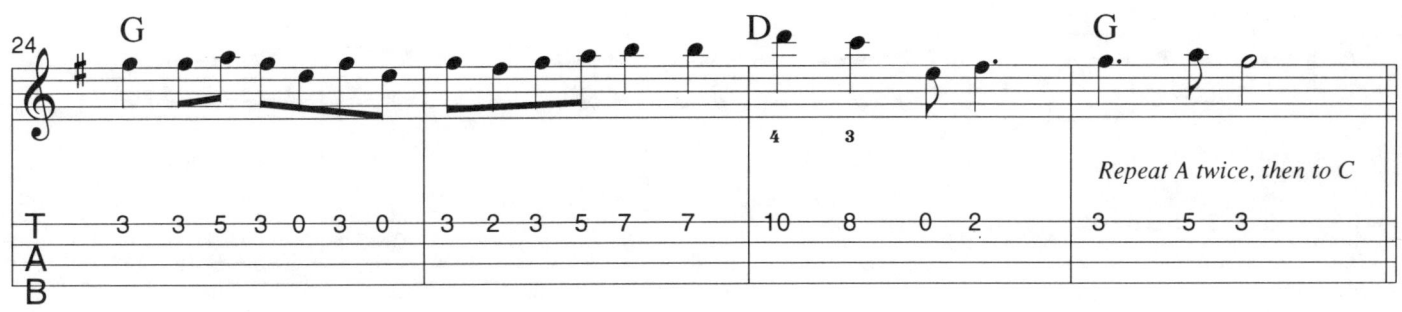

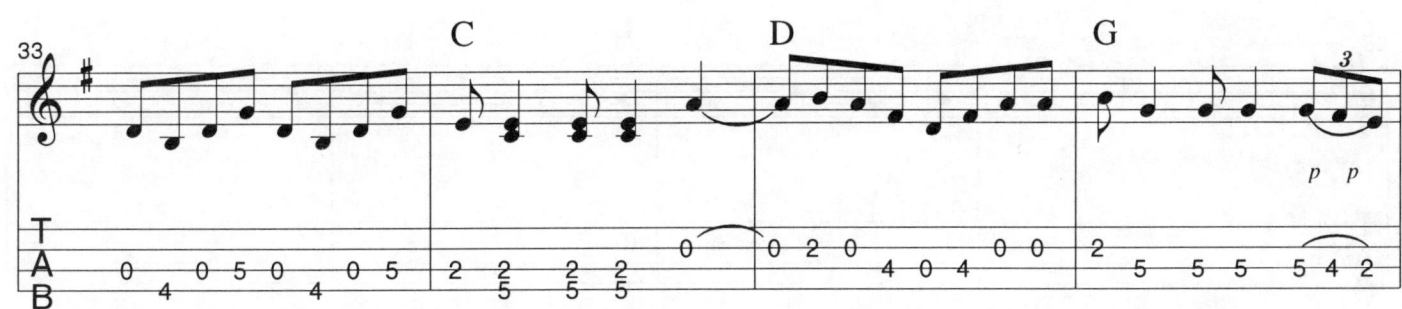
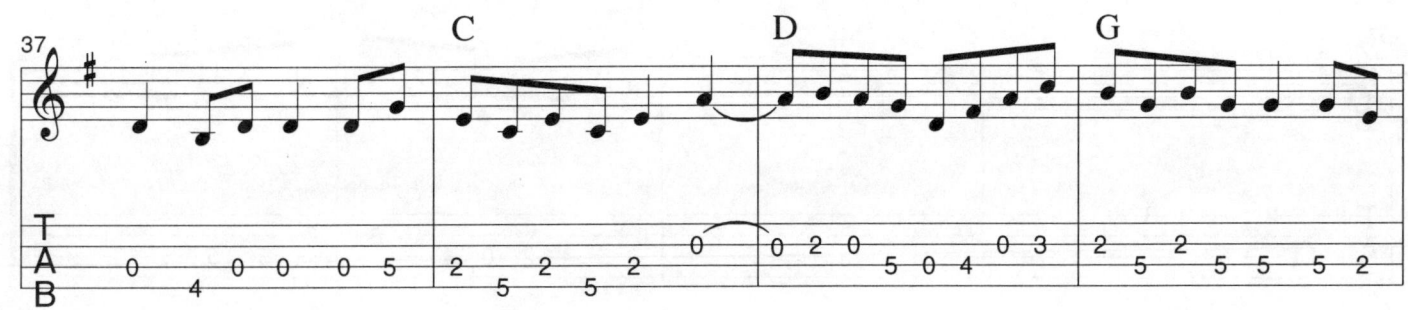

Dance All Night Mando 2

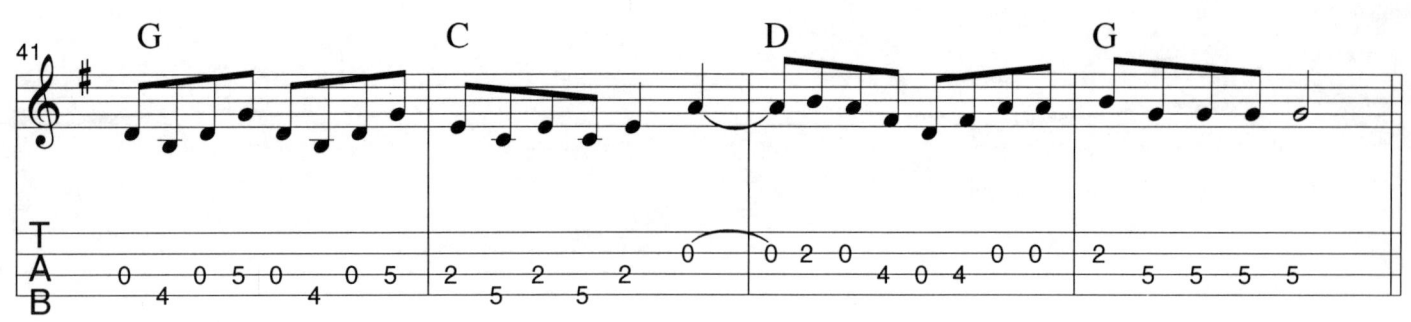
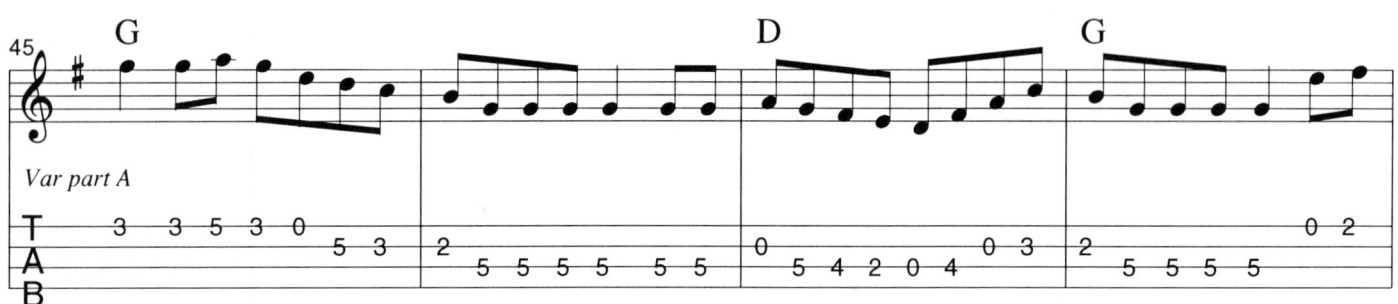

Var part A

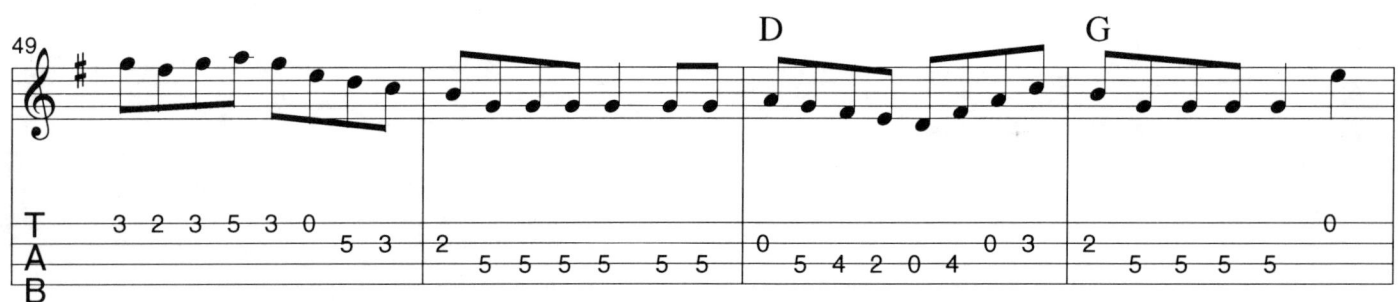
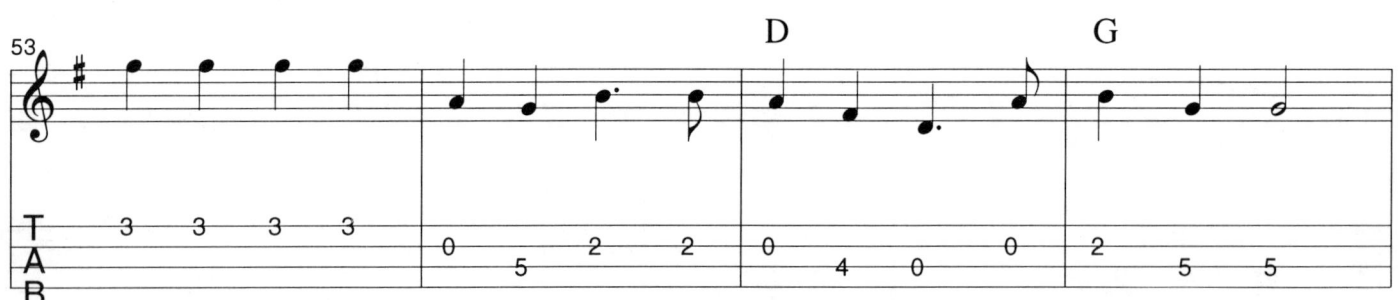
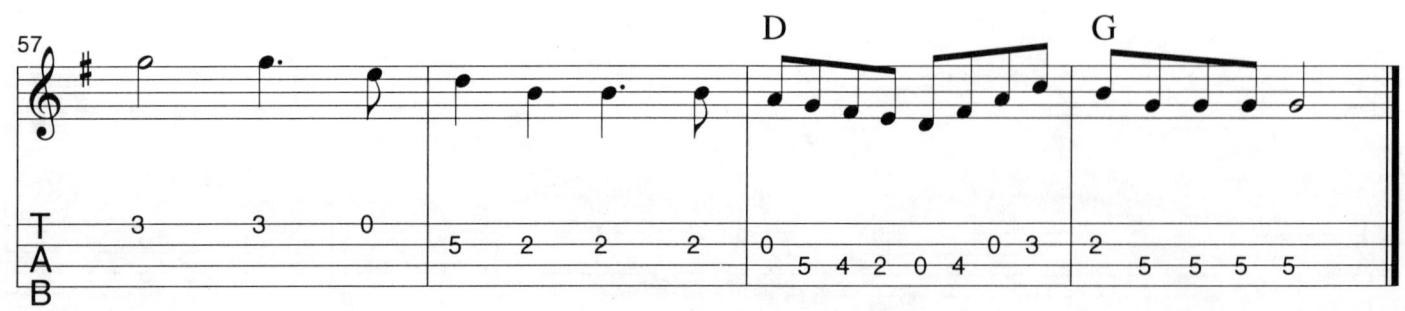

This page has been left blank to avoid awkward page turns

You Ain't Talking to Me

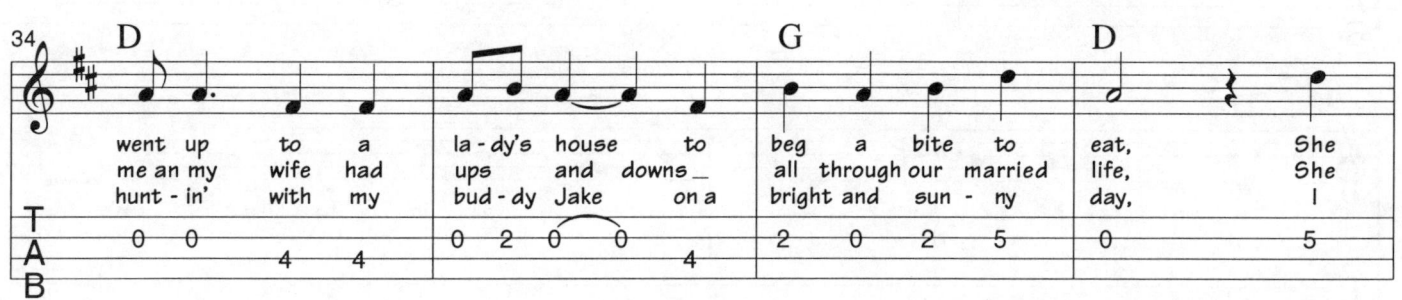

You Ain't Talking to Me Mando 2

This page has been left blank to avoid awkward page turns

Money Musk

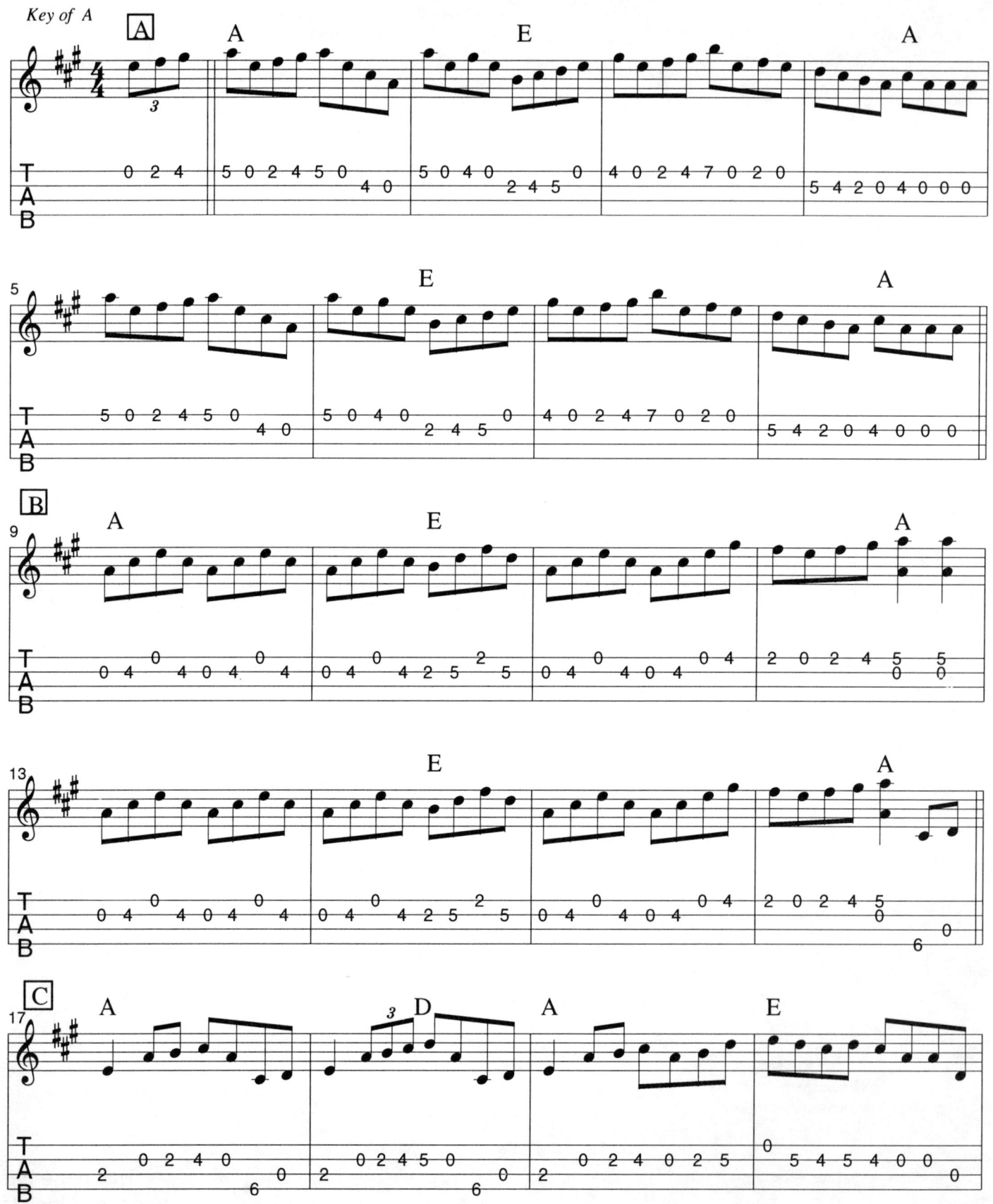

Money Musk Mando 1

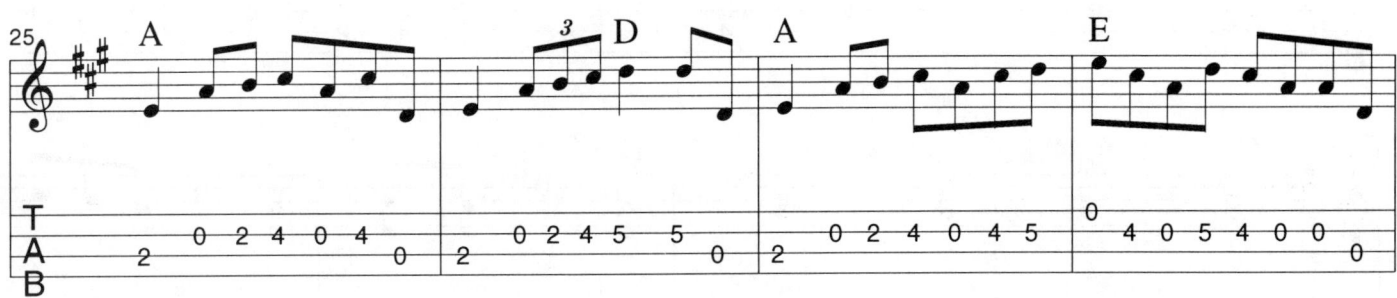

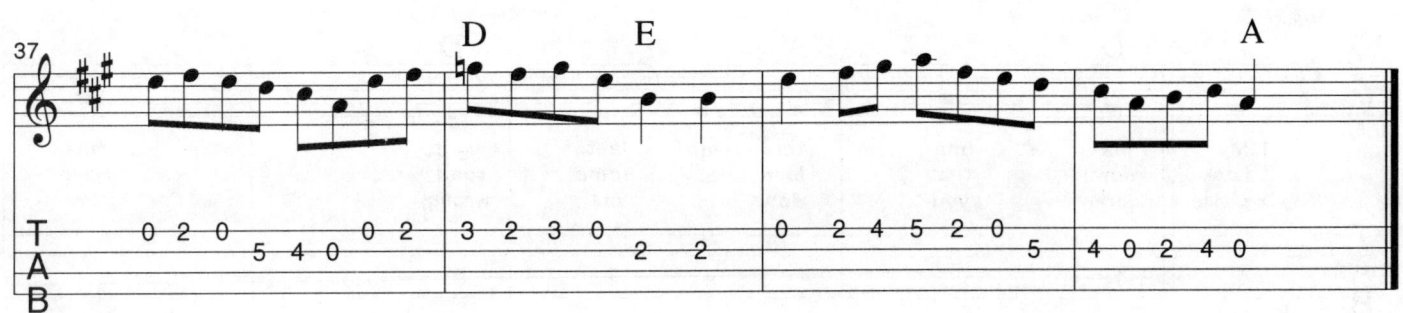

Money Musk Mando 2

There's More Pretty Girls Than One

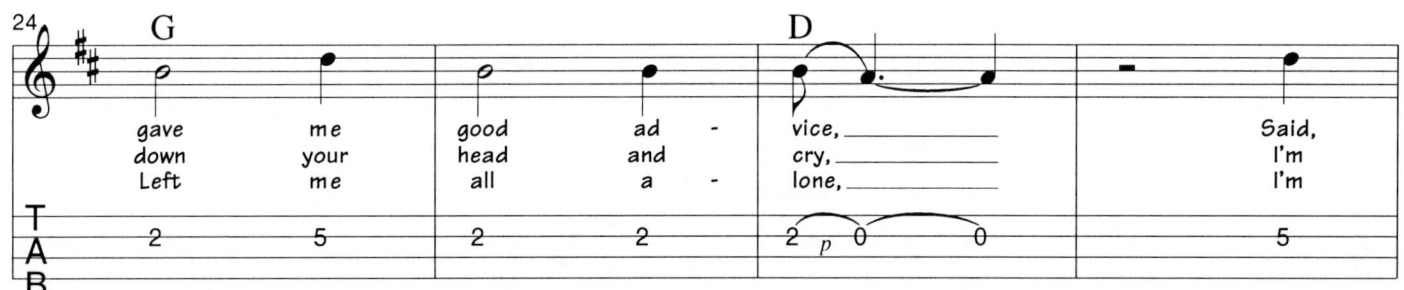
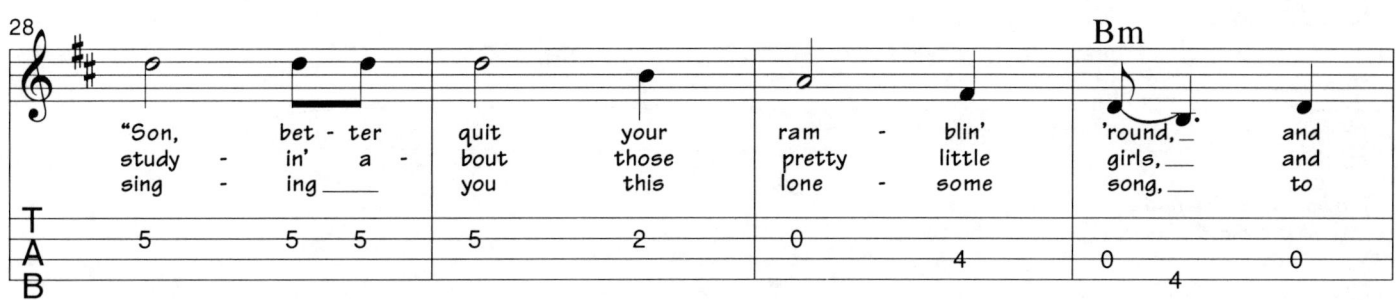

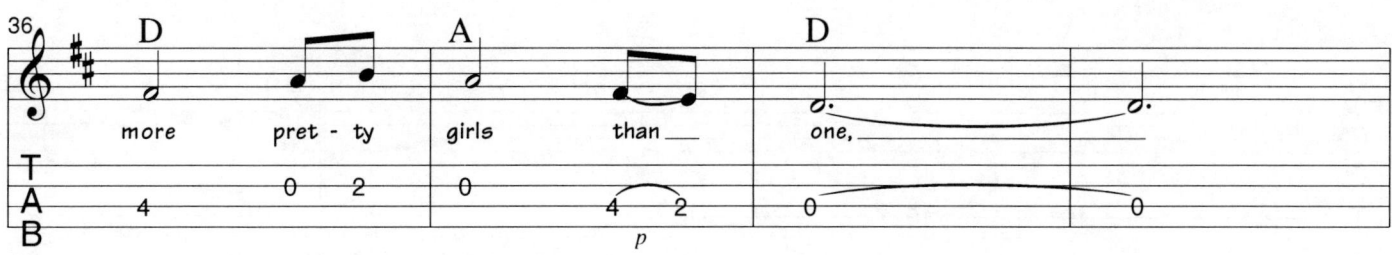
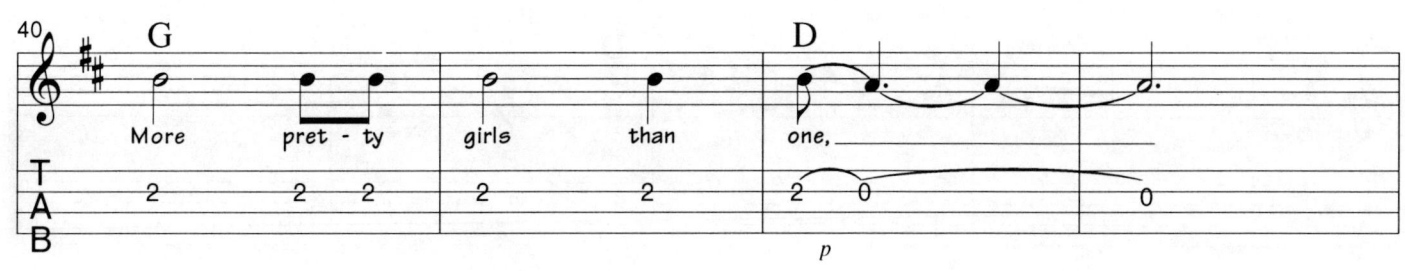

There's More Pretty Girls Than One Mando 2

This page has been left blank to avoid awkward page turns

Fire on the Mountain

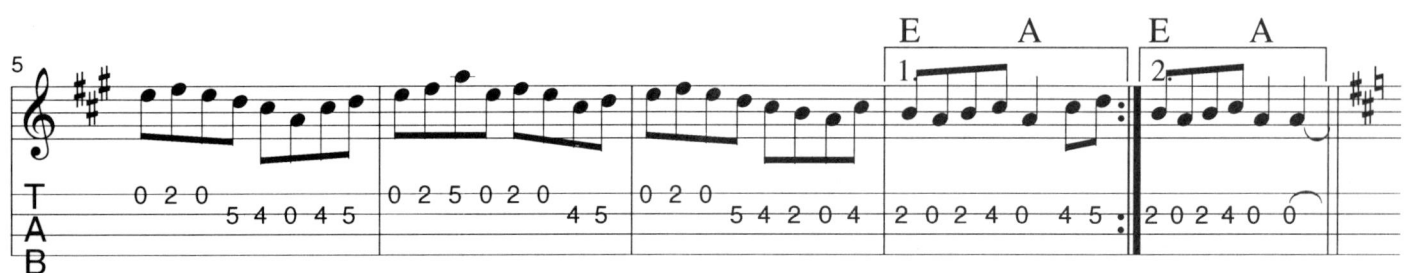

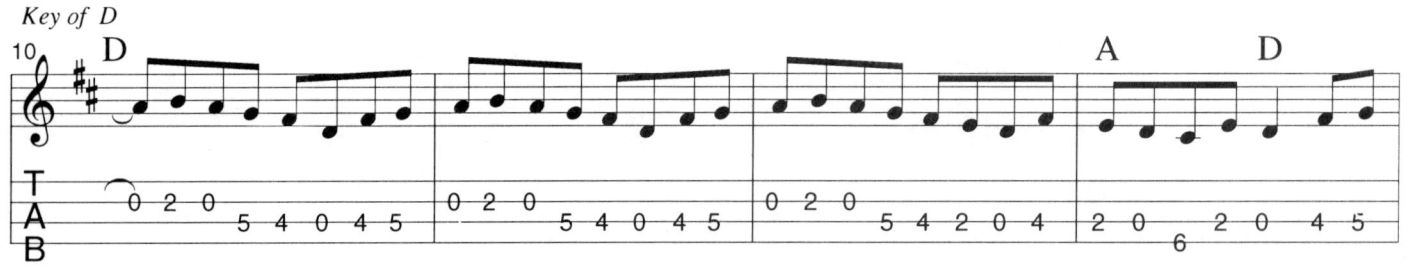

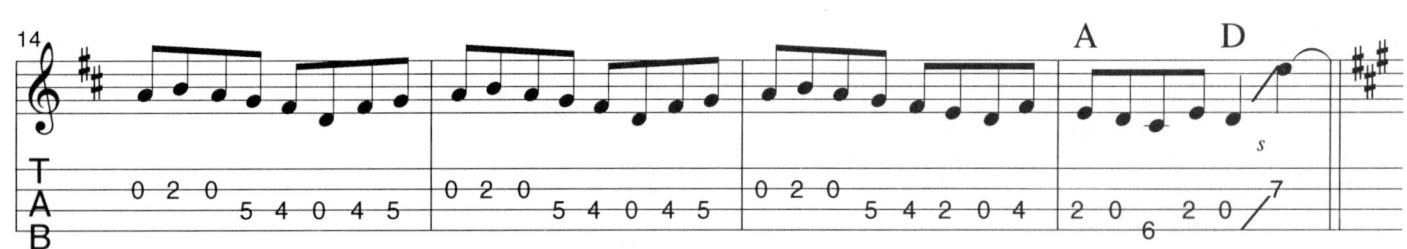

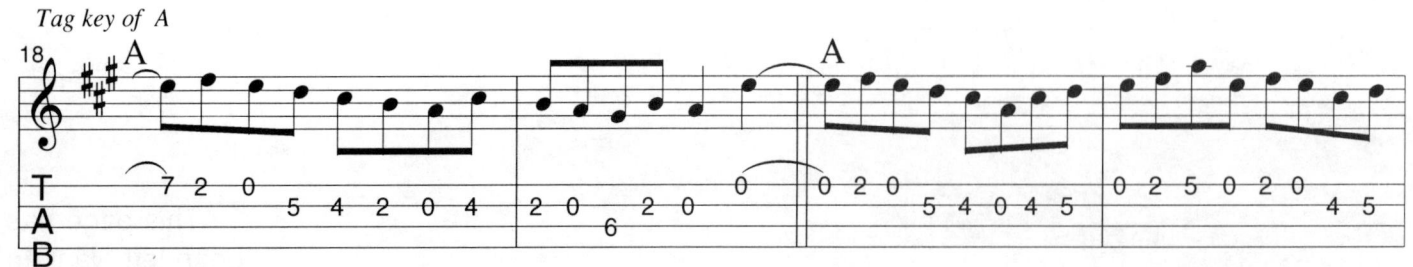

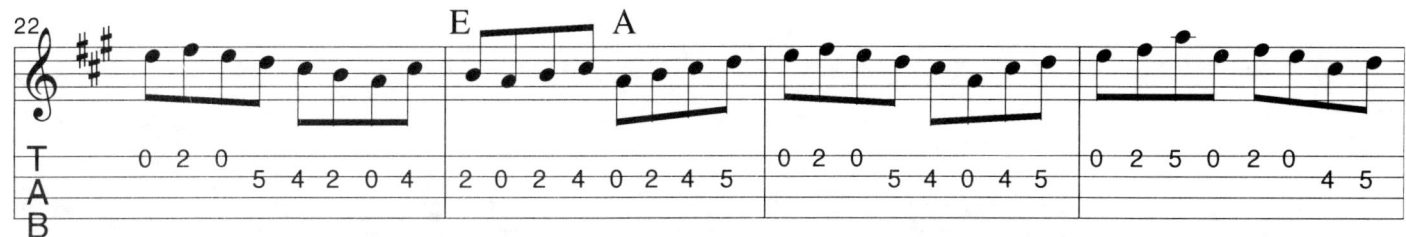

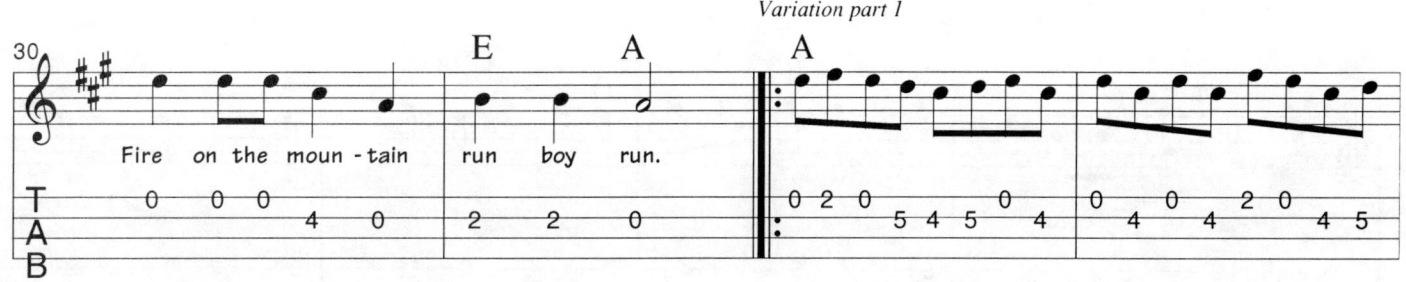
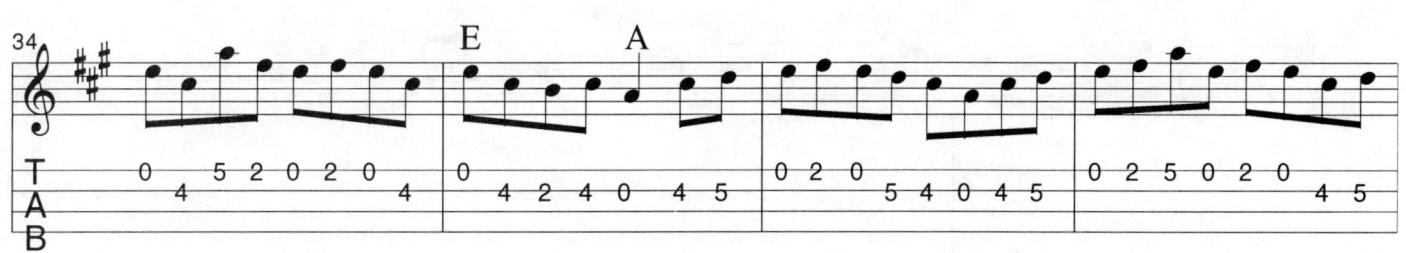

Fire on the Mountain Mando 2

Gypsy Girl

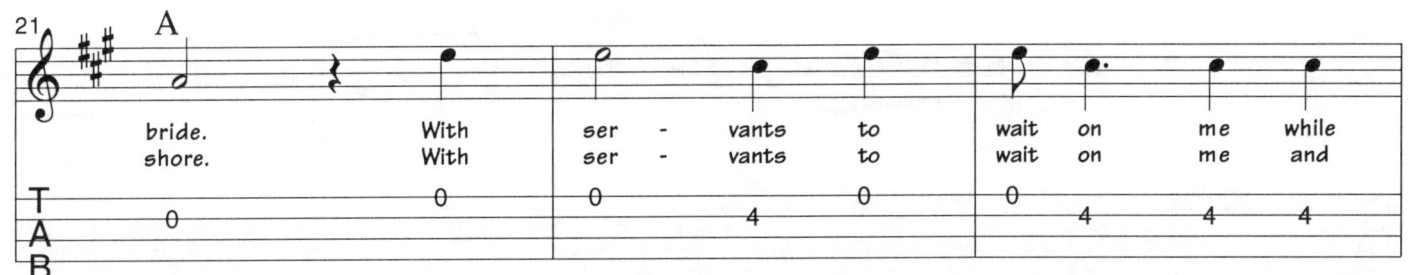

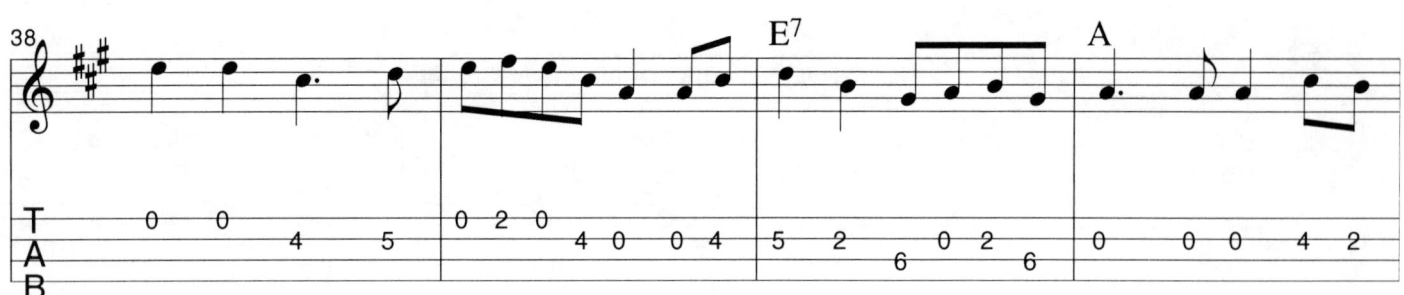

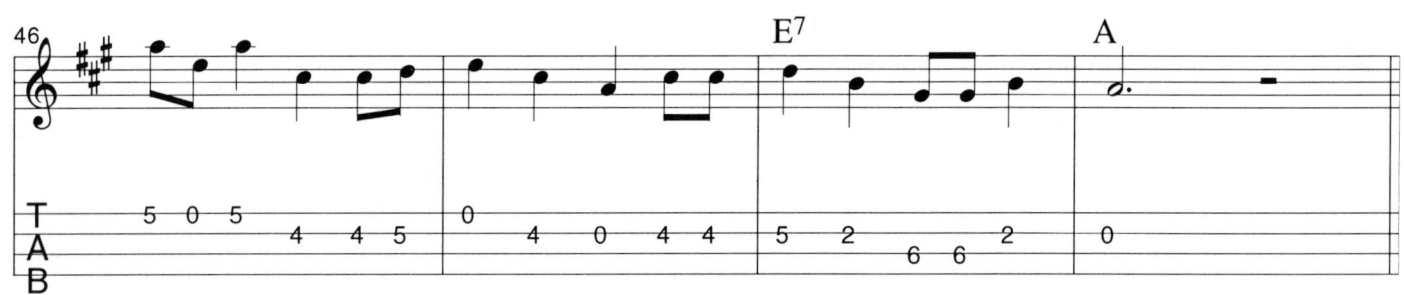
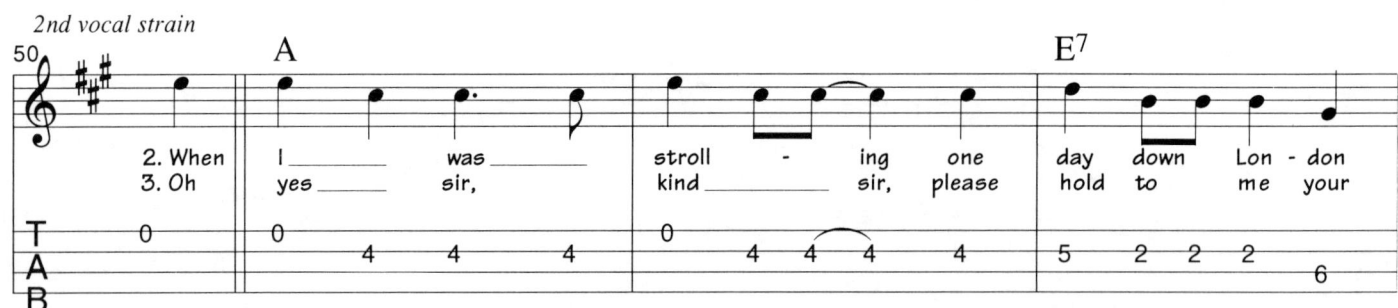
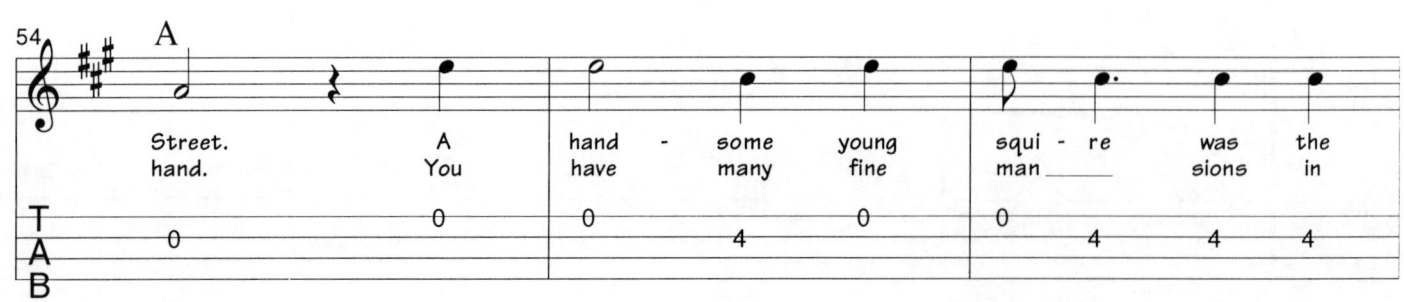

Pig Ankle Rag

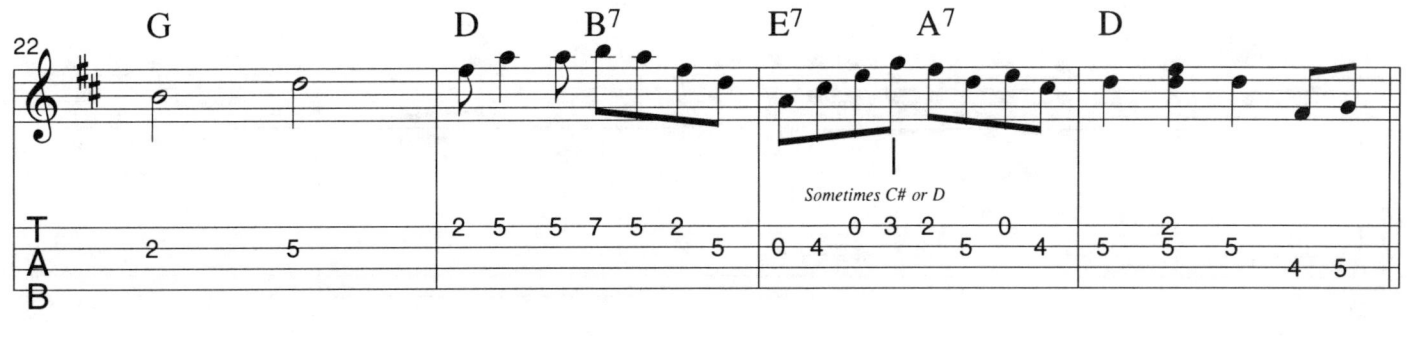

Part B.2

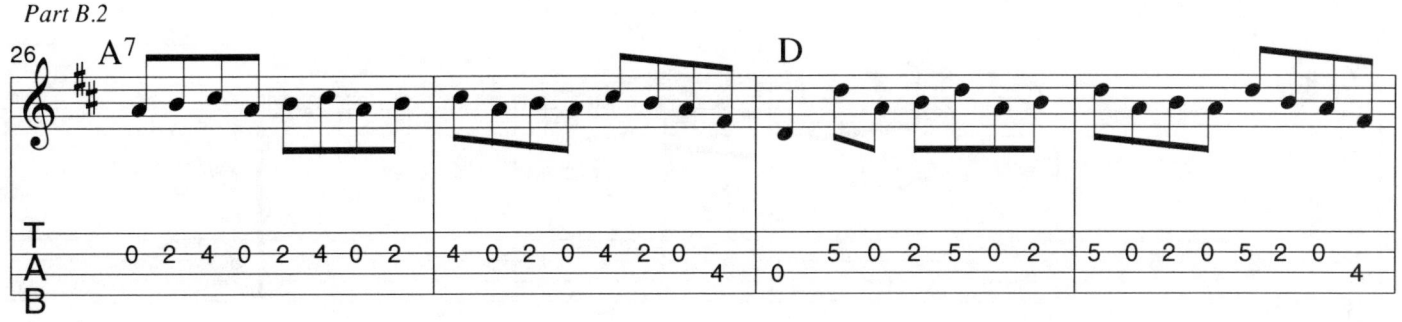

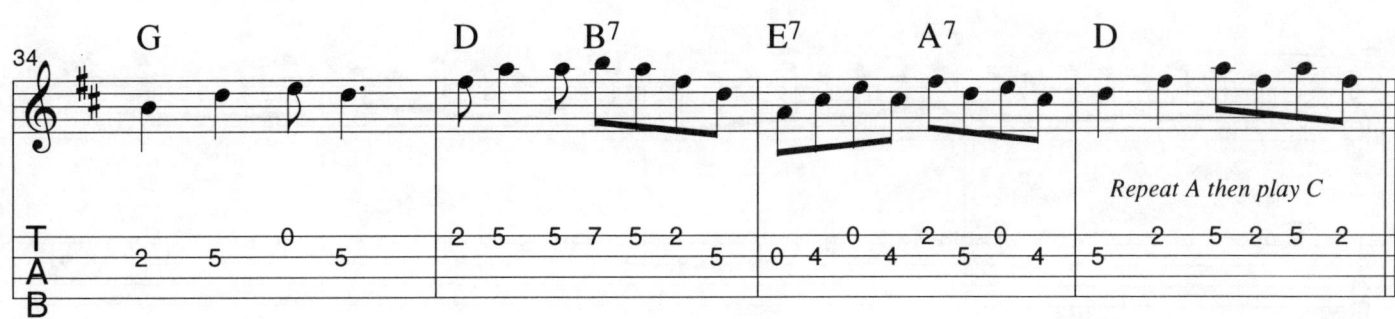

Part C

Pig Ankle Rag Mando 2

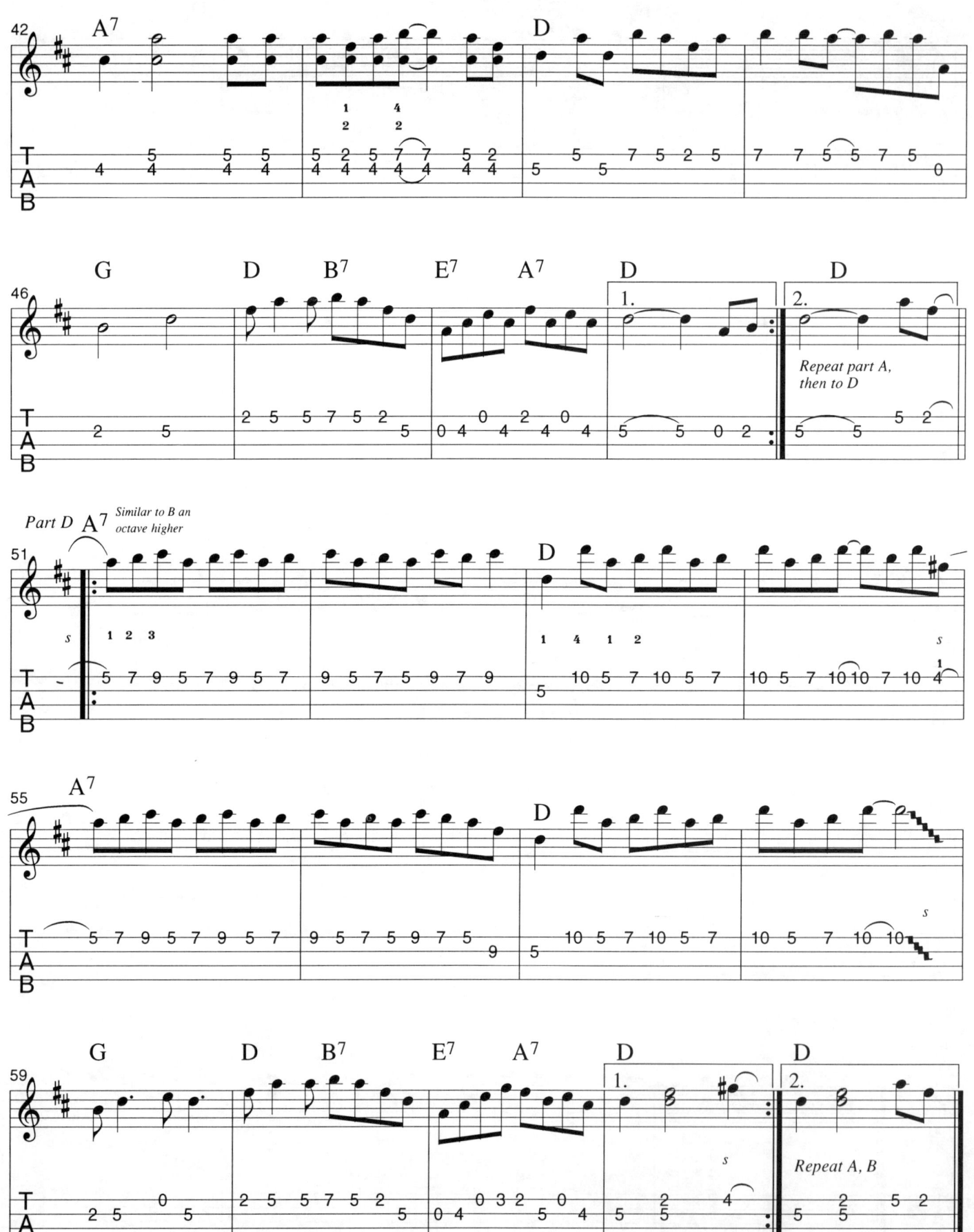

Wild Bill Jones

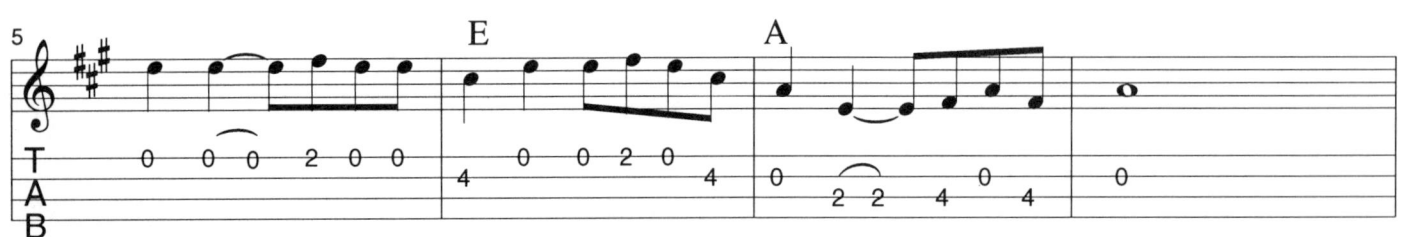
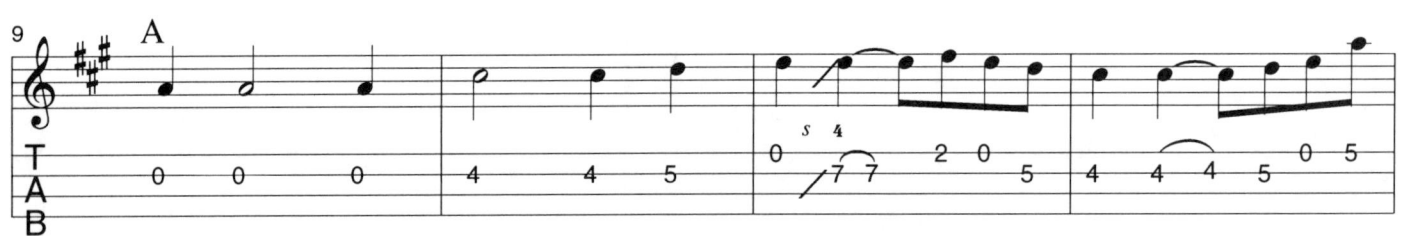
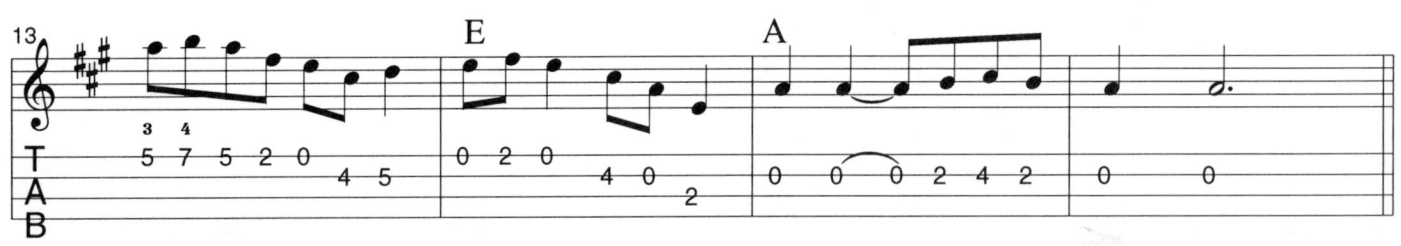
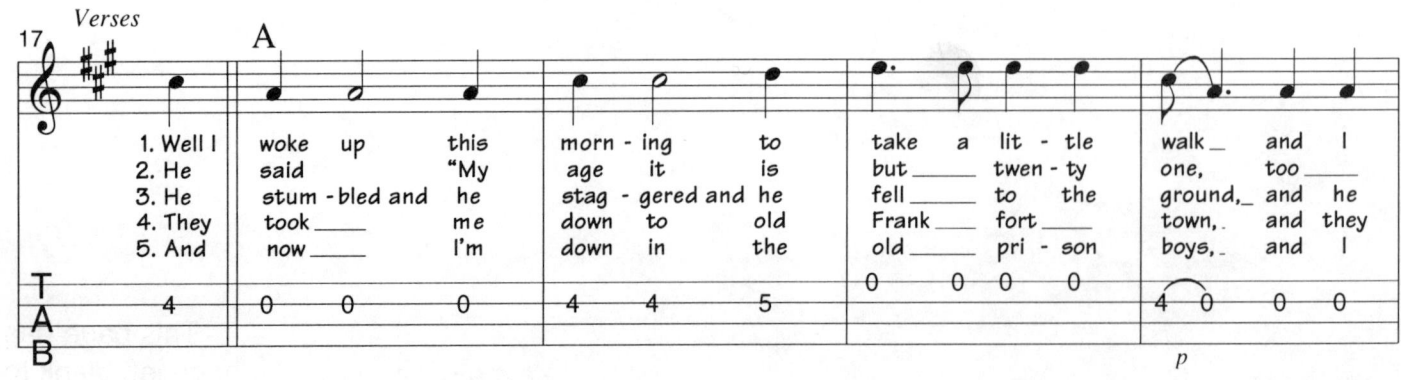

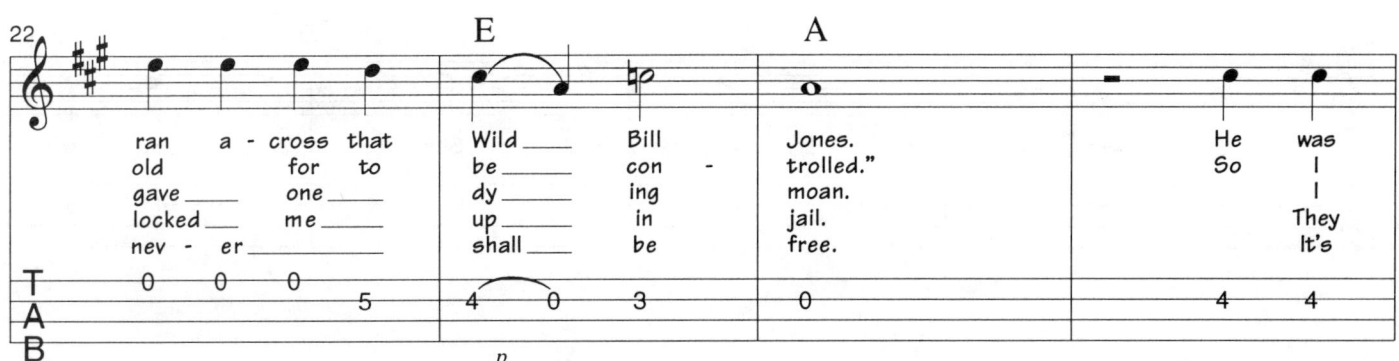

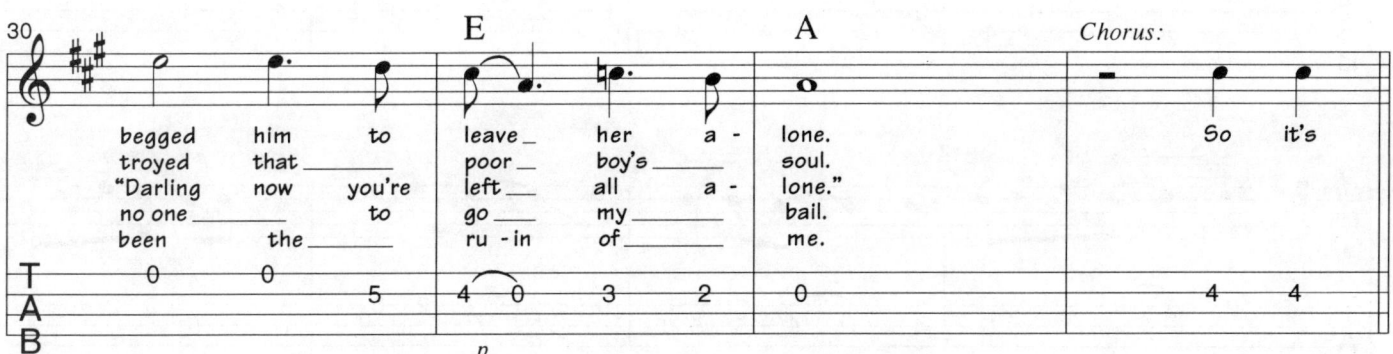

Wild Bill Jones 2

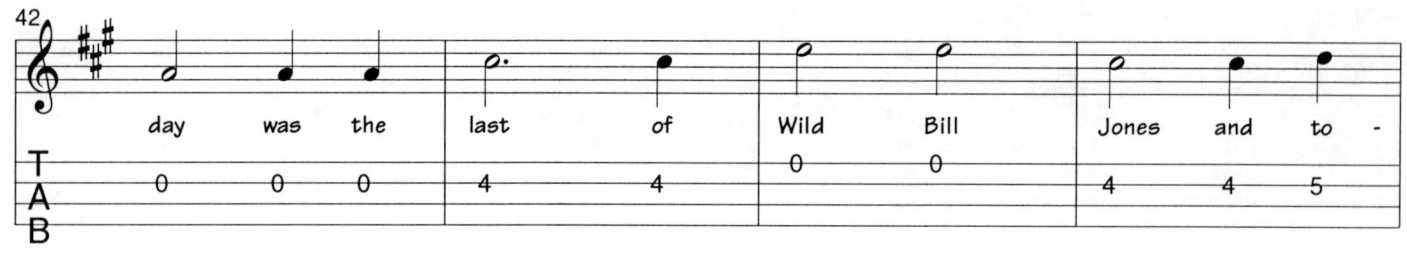
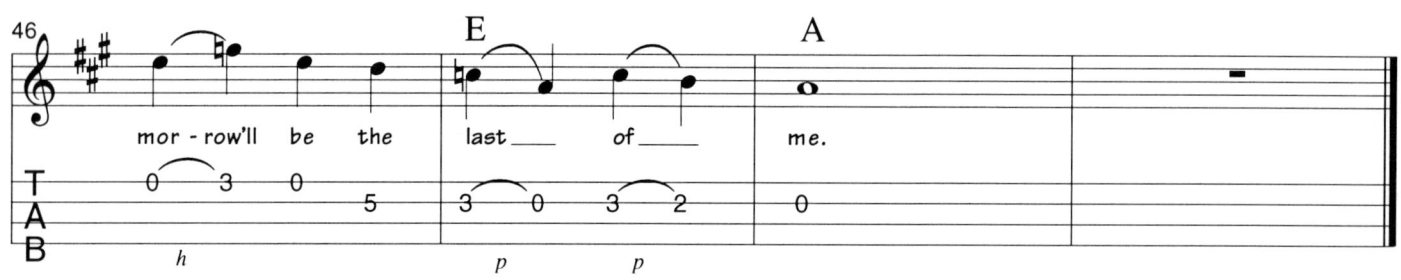

Fiddle 1

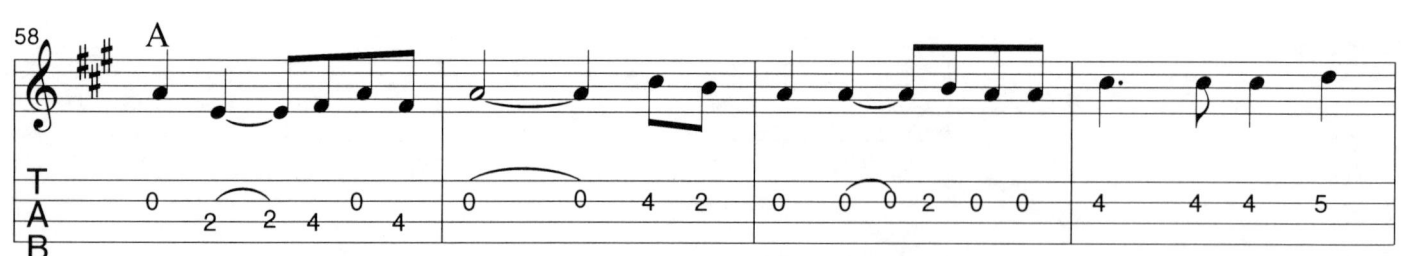

Wild Bill Jones 3

Wild Bill Jones 4

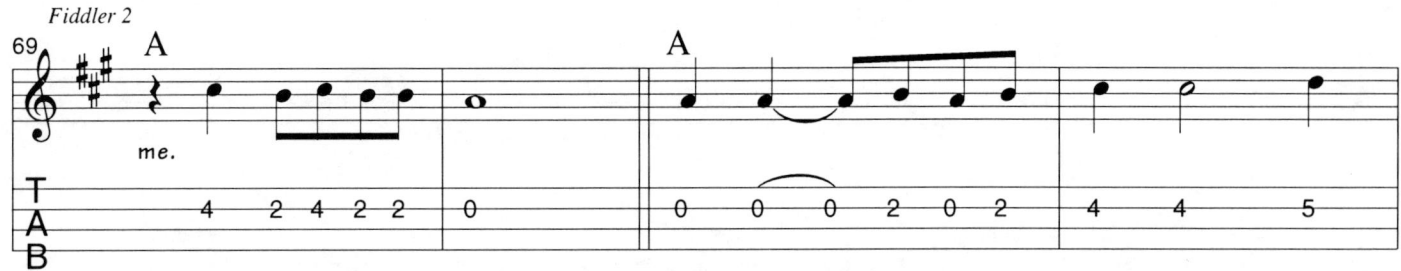

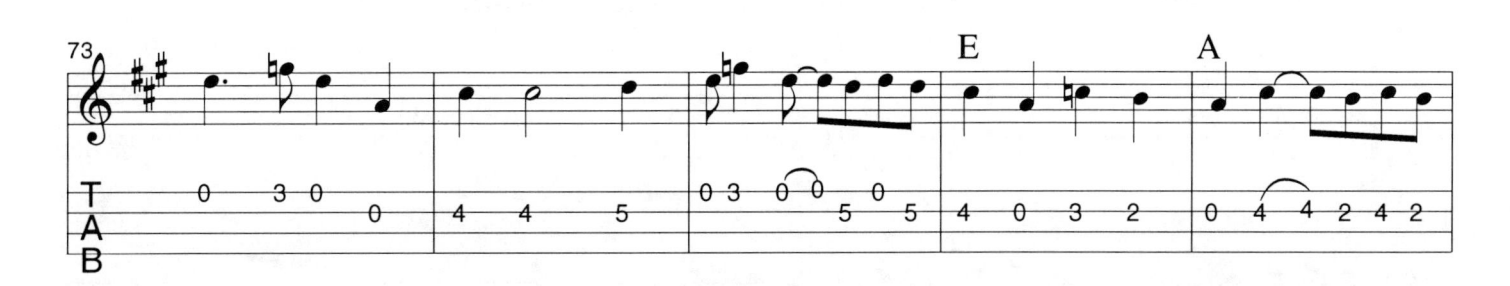

Sleeping Lulu

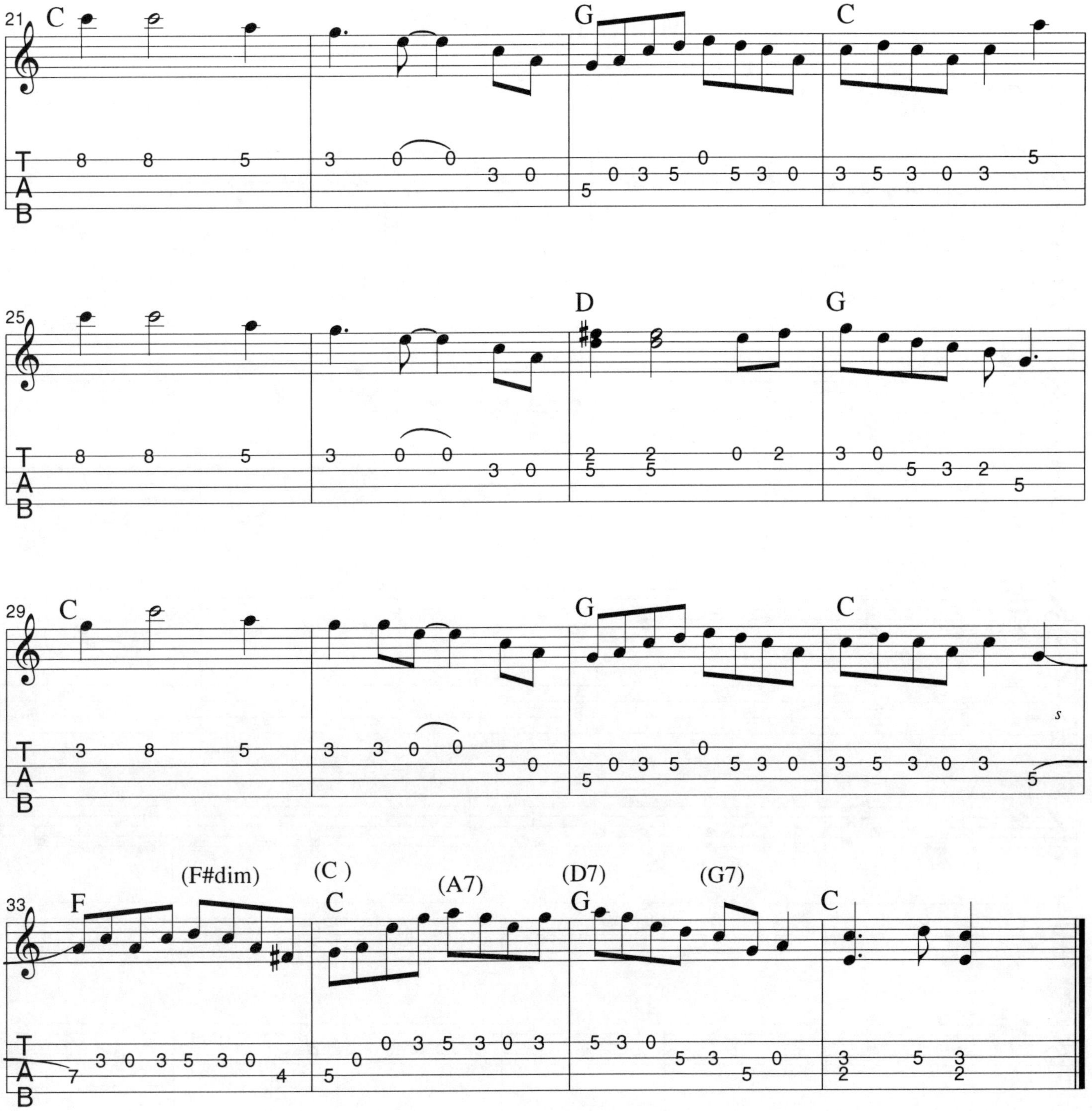
21 C G C
TAB
25 D G
TAB
29 C G C
TAB
33 F (F#dim) (C) C (A7) (D7) G (G7) C
TAB

Meeting in the Air

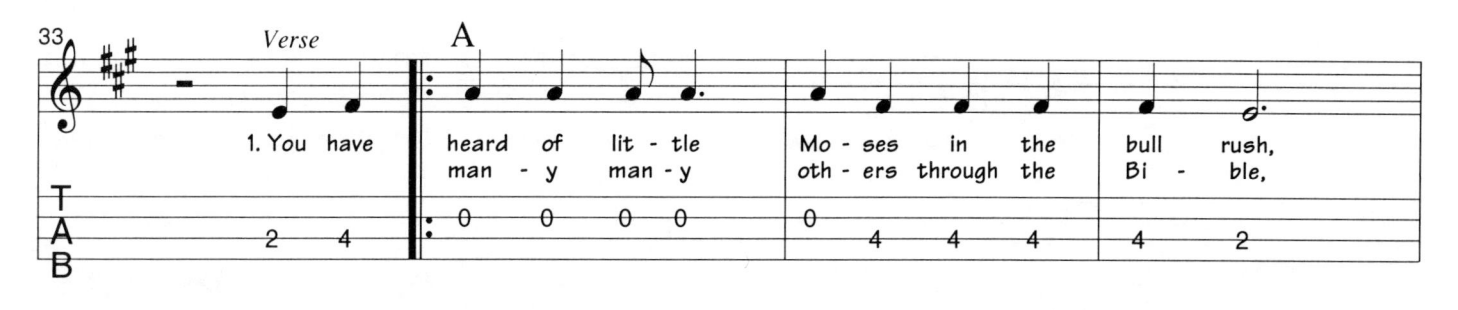

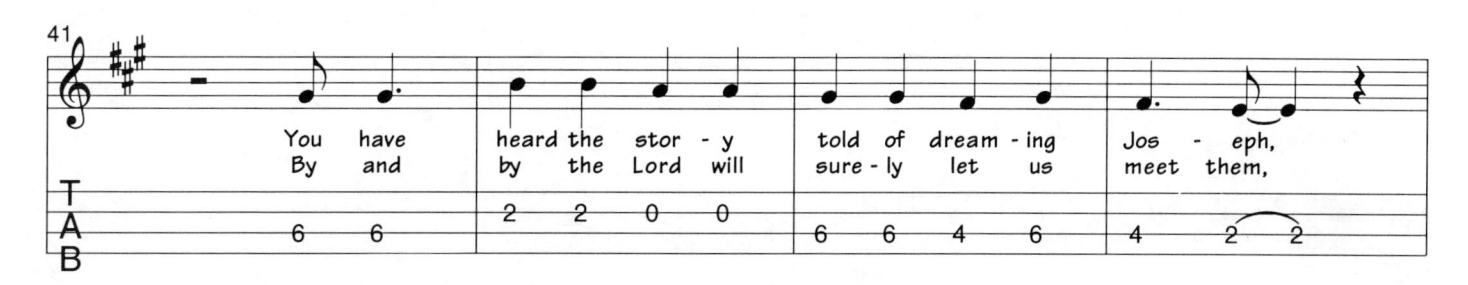

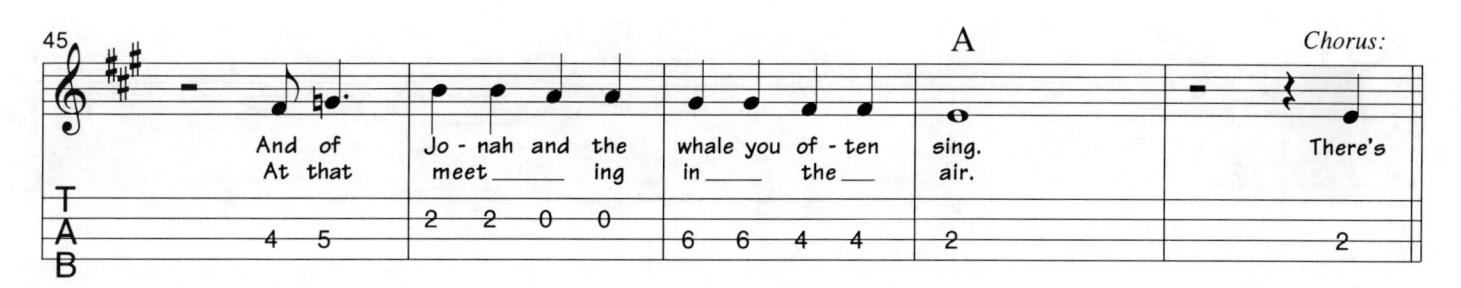

Meeting in the Air 2

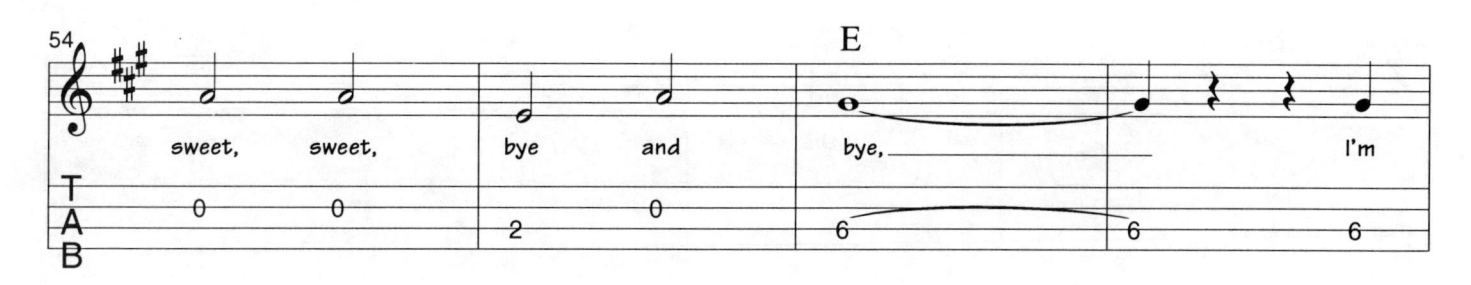

41

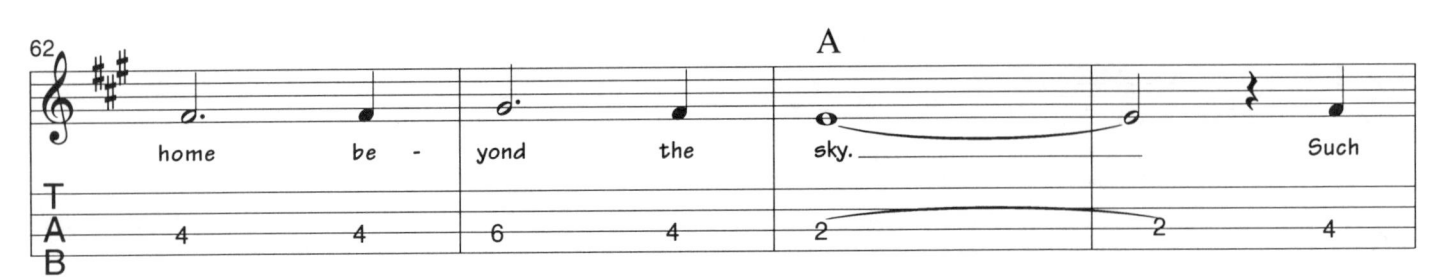

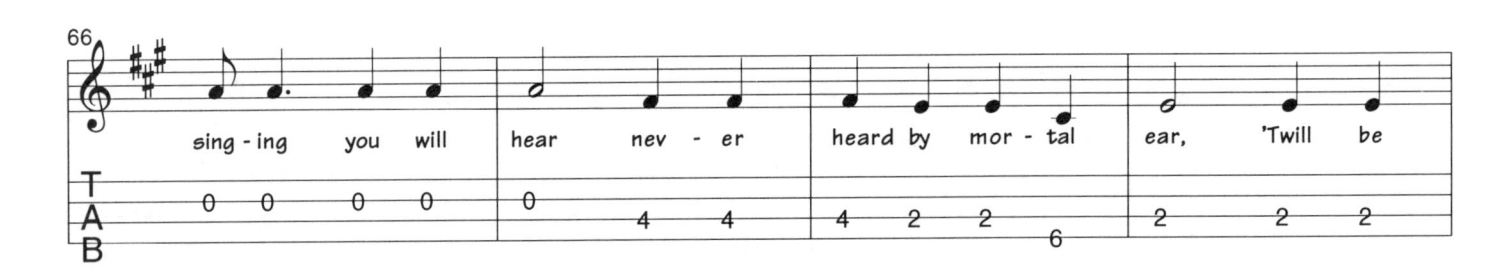

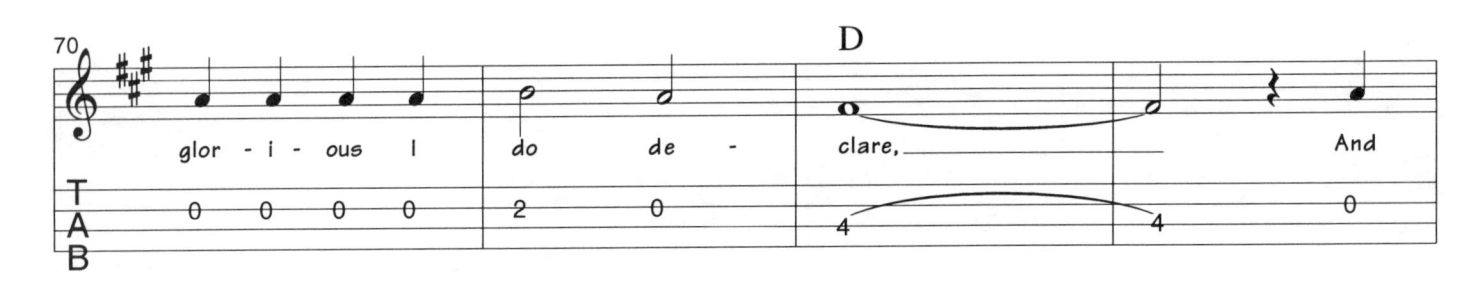

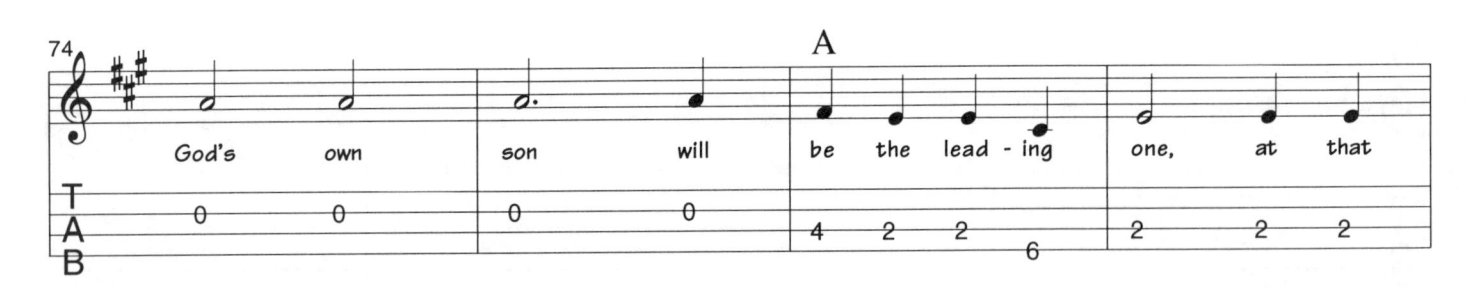

Meeting in the Air

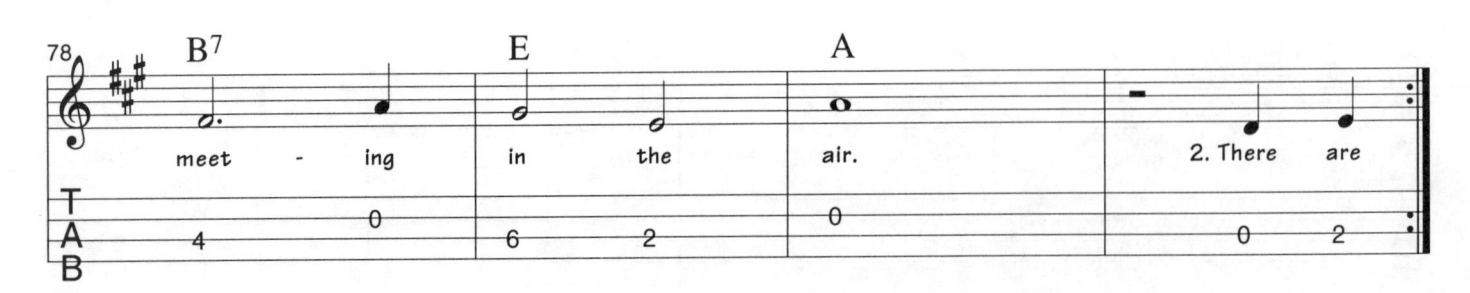

Meeting in the Air 4

Meeting in the Air

This page has been left blank to avoid awkward page turns

Hawks and Eagles

Key of D
Intro based on fiddle

Part 1 var

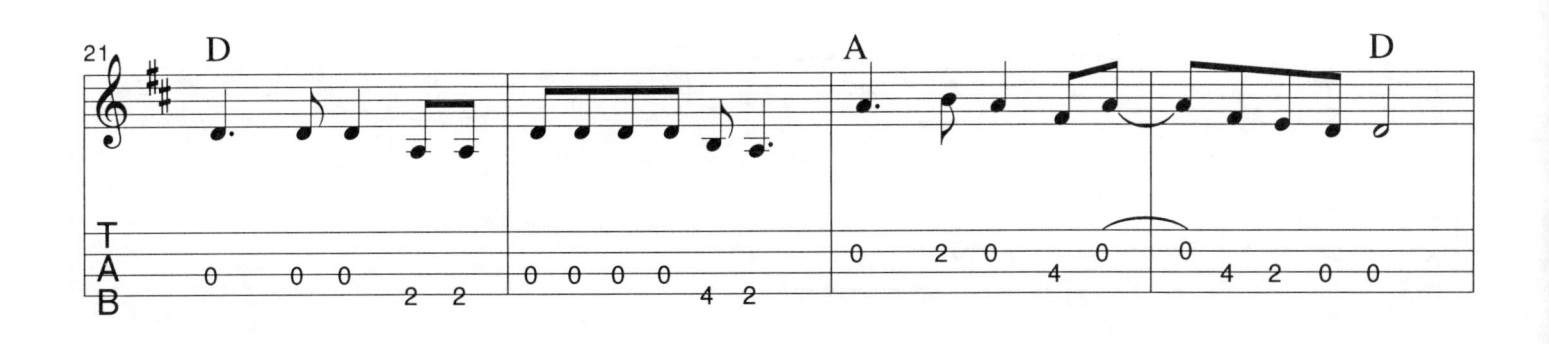

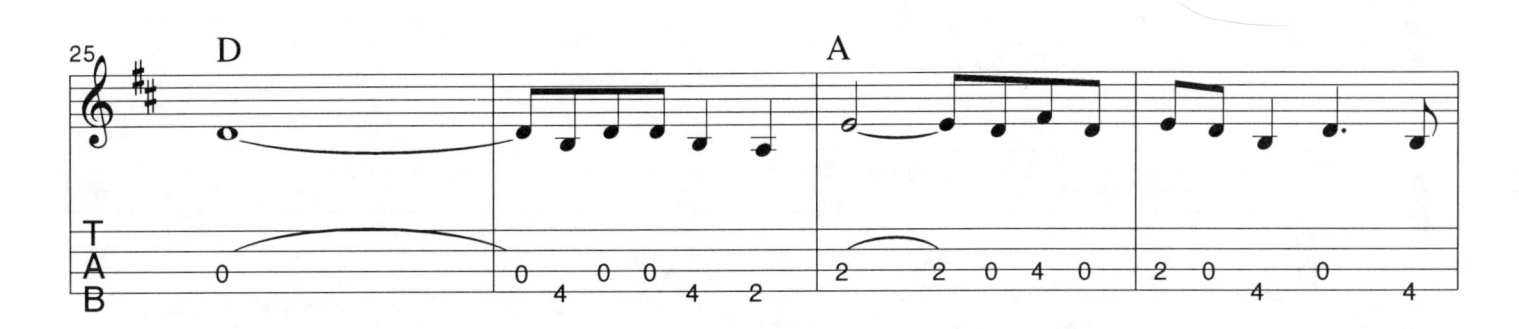

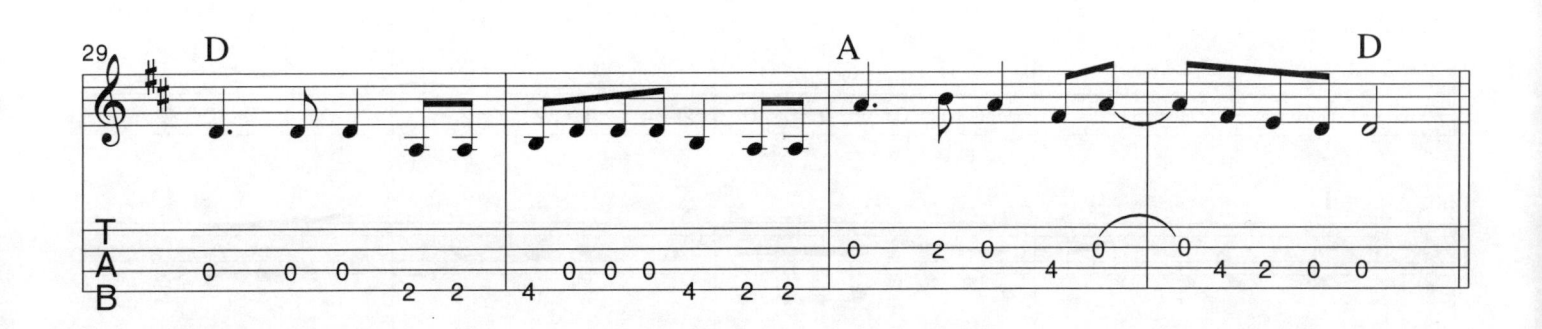

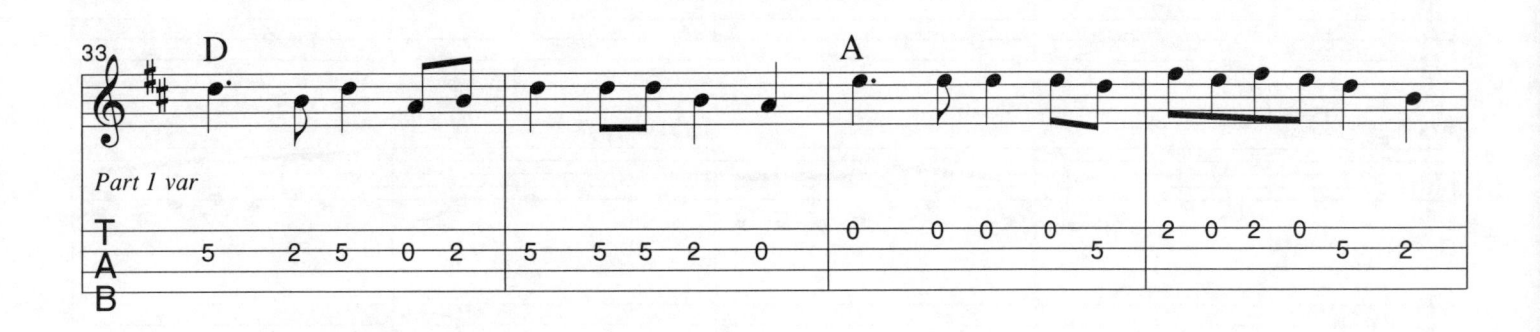

Hawks and Eagles Mando 2

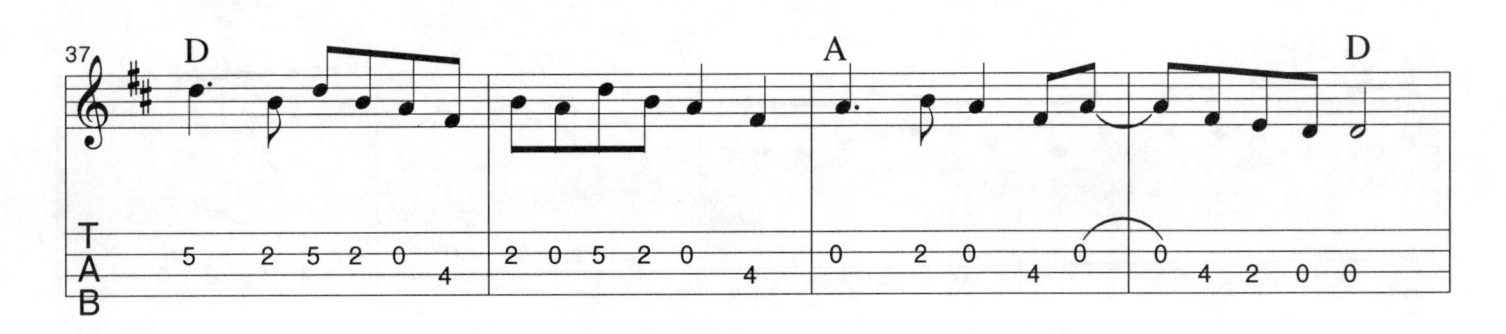

Hawks and Eagles Mando 3

48

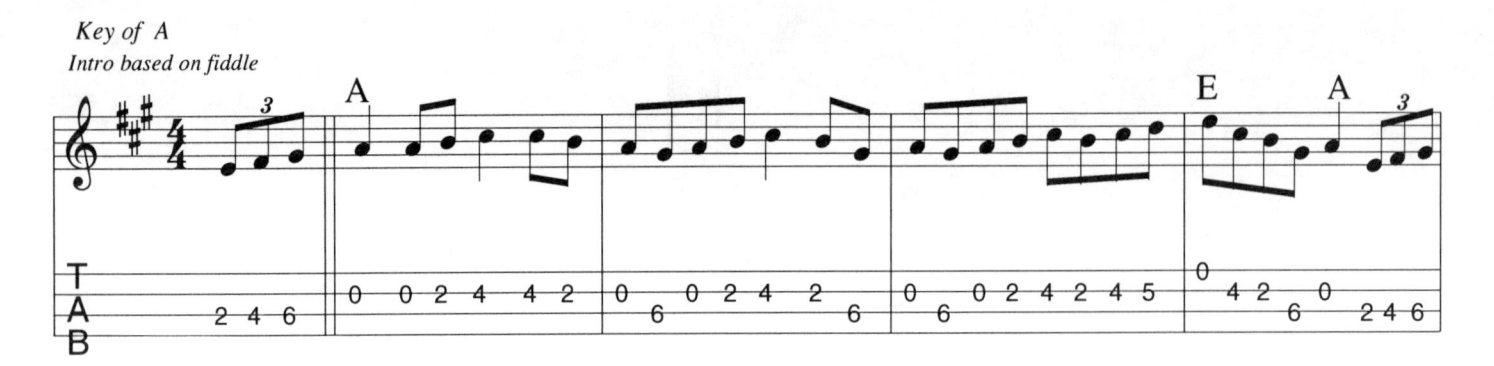

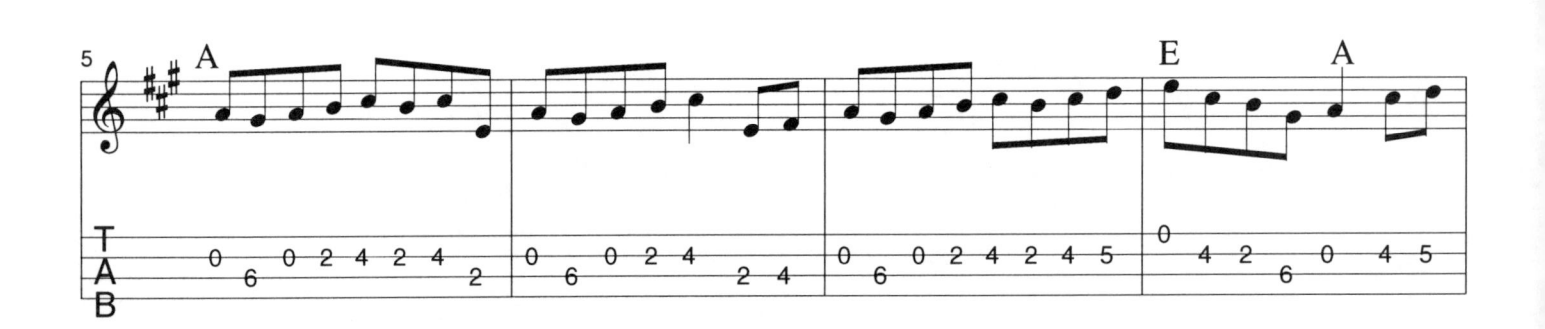

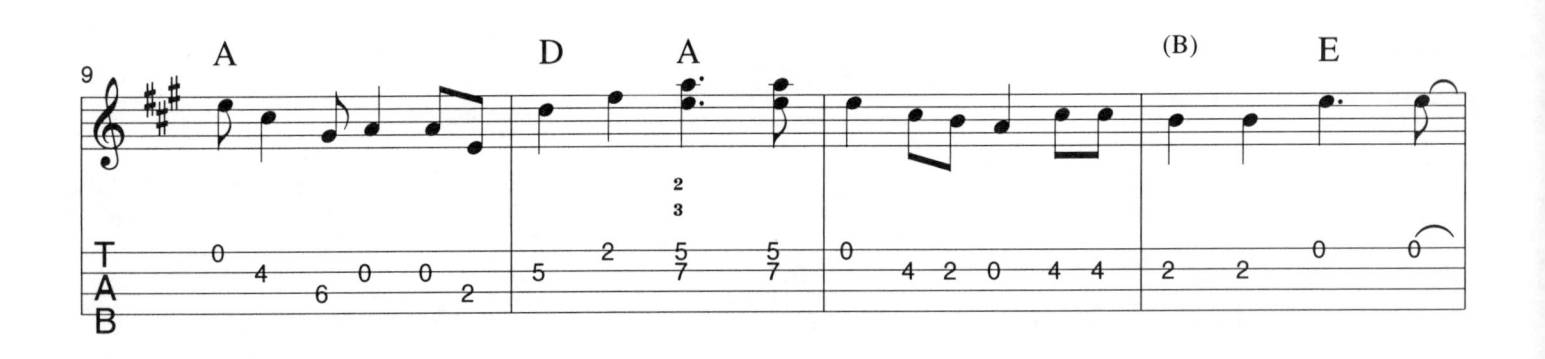

Who Broke the Lock

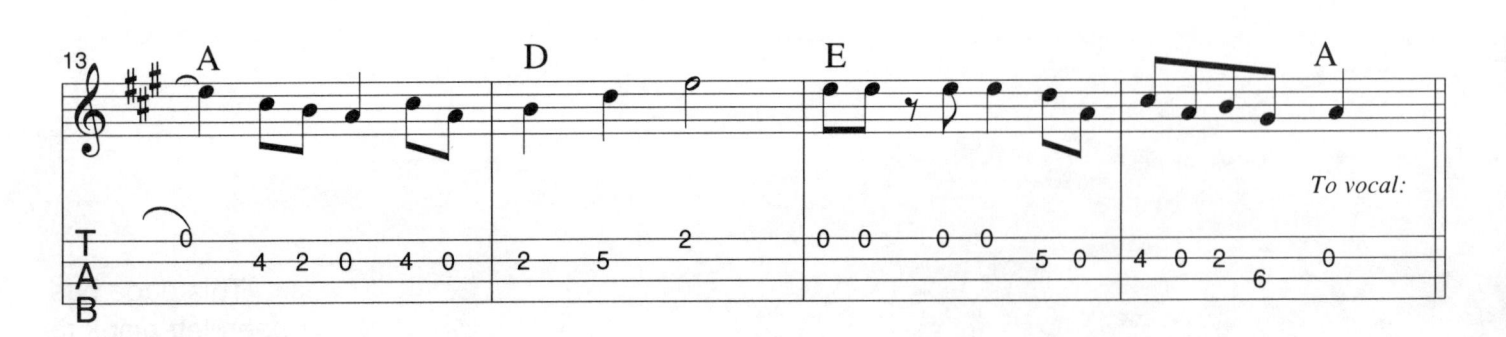

Key of A
Intro based on fiddle

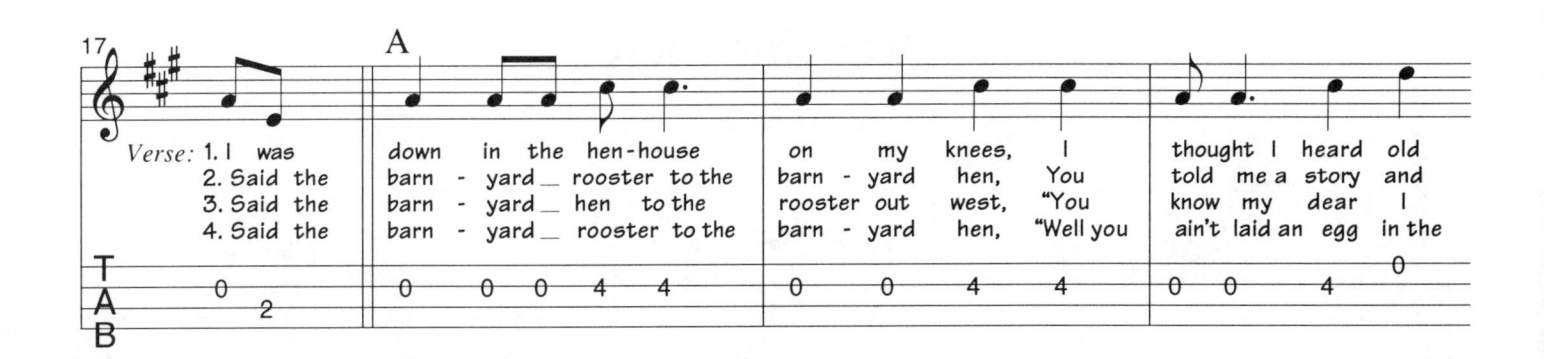

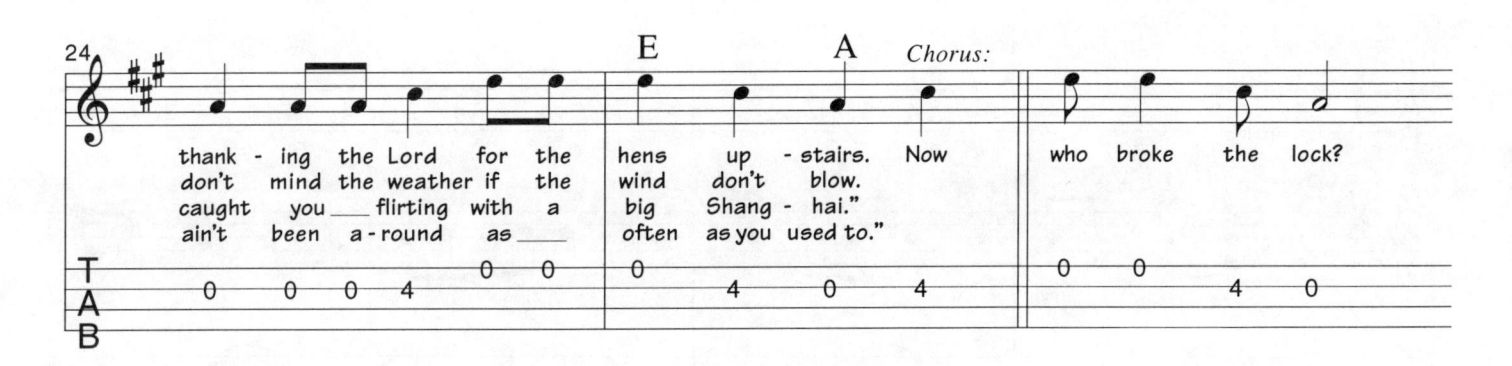

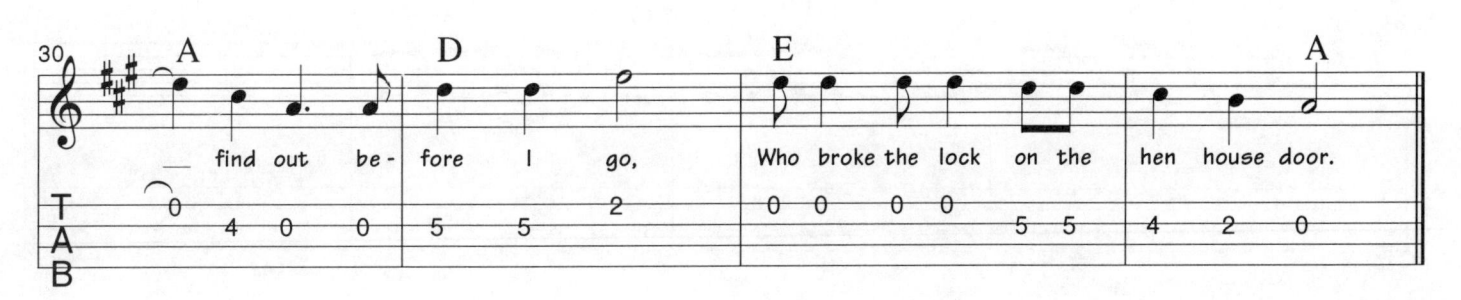

Verse:
1. I was down in the hen-house on my knees, I thought I heard old Bruno sneeze, It was nothing but the rooster saying his prayers, He was thanking the Lord for the hens upstairs. Now who broke the lock?
2. Said the barnyard rooster to the barnyard hen, You told me a story and I know when, You told me that Sally made her cakes all dough, And I don't mind the weather if the wind don't blow.
3. Said the barnyard hen to the rooster out west, "You know my dear I love you the best," Said the barnyard rooster "You're telling me a lie, 'Cause I caught you flirting with a big Shanghai."
4. Said the barnyard rooster to the barnyard hen, "Well you ain't laid an egg in the Lord knows when." Said the barnyard hen to the barnyard rooster, "Well you ain't been around as often as you used to."

Chorus:
I don't know, Who broke the lock on the hen house door? I'll find out before I go, Who broke the lock on the hen house door.

Who Broke the Lock Mando 2

Way Out There

Key of D
Intro based on fiddle

25
D
A7
1. A lone - ly spot I know where no man will
2. As she pulled out of sight I ___ looked to my
3. So I threw down my load on that des - ert
4. So I closed my eyes to the star - ry
5. As ___ she was passing by I ___ caught her on the
29
D
go, Where the shad - ows have all the room, ___ I was
right, To my left and ___ eve - ry where, ___ But ___
road, And I rest - ed my wea - ry legs, ___ Watched the
skies, and I lost ___ my self in dreams, ___ Dreamed the
fly, I ___ climbed in an o - pen door, ___ Then I
34
A7
D
rid - ing free on that old S. P. a -
all I could see was a cac - tus tree and a
sink - ing sun make the tall shadows run out a -
des - ert sand was a milk and honey land and I
looked all a - round to that des - ert ground saw the
38
E
A7
hum - ming a south - ern tune, ___ When a
prairie dog ___ play - ing there, ___ Saw a
cross the ___ bar - ren plain, ___ Then I
woke up ___ with a start, ___ There's a
spot I would see no more, ___ As I
42
D
G
Fifth verse To Coda
man come a - long made me hush my song, Kicked me
prairie dog ___ feed on a tum - ble weed, That's his
hummed ___ a tune to that ris - ing moon, It gets
train com - ing back on that one way track, Gon - na
rode ___ a - way I heard that pale moon say, "Fare thee
T
A
B

46
D
A7
D
off a way out ___ there.
home a way out ___ there.
lone - some way out ___ there.
take me way from ___ here.
Verses 1-4 to Chorus
p
Coda
50
D
A7
D
well, pal, sure gets lone - some here." ___
Chorus:
56
G
(G♭)
(G)
Woo ___ Woo - ooo yo - dee
62
D
A7
aye - eee he ___ Hooo ___
68
(A♭)
(A)
D
Oh - he aye - he he. ___

This page has been left blank to avoid awkward page turns

Carroll County Blues

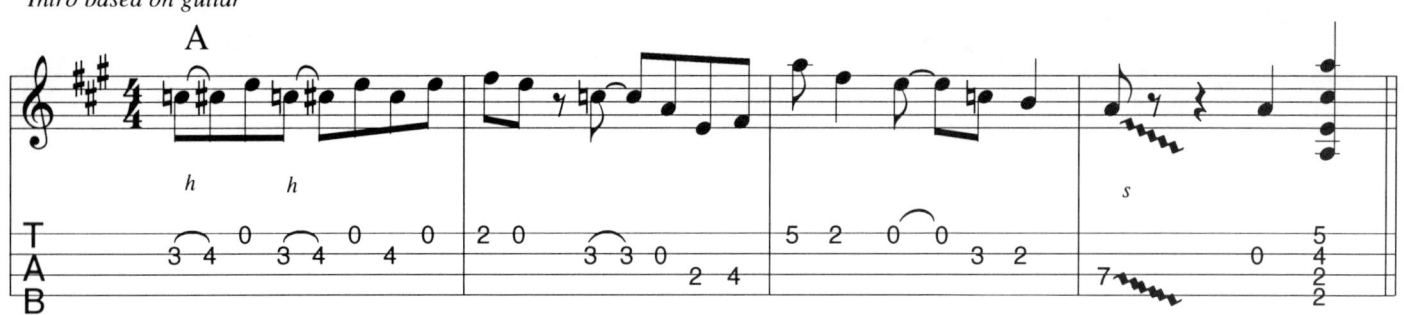

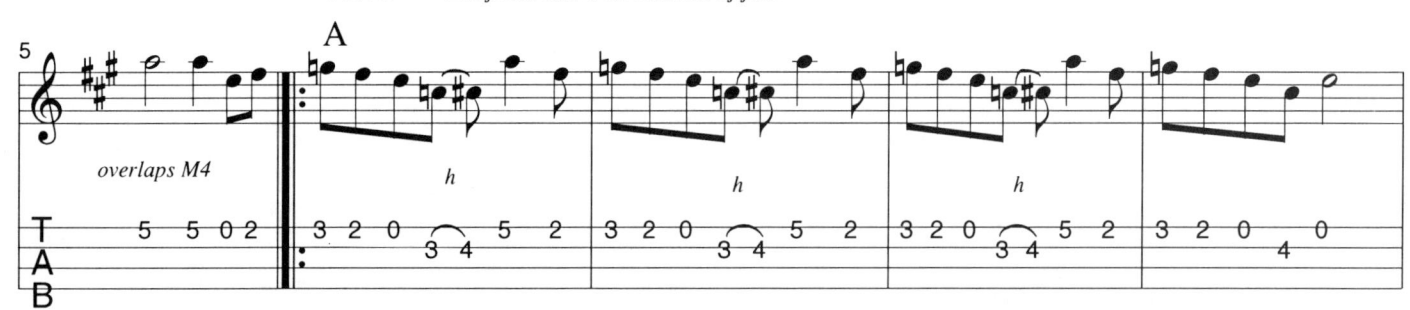

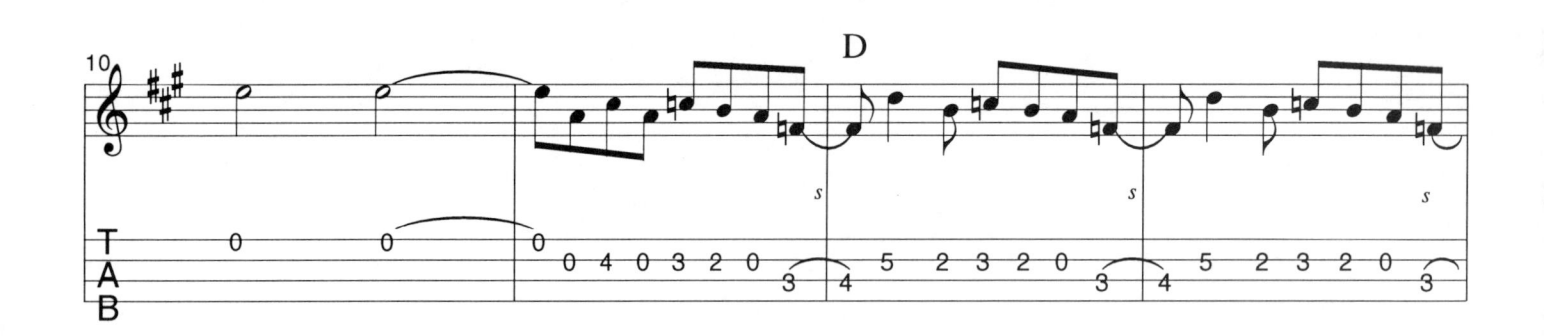

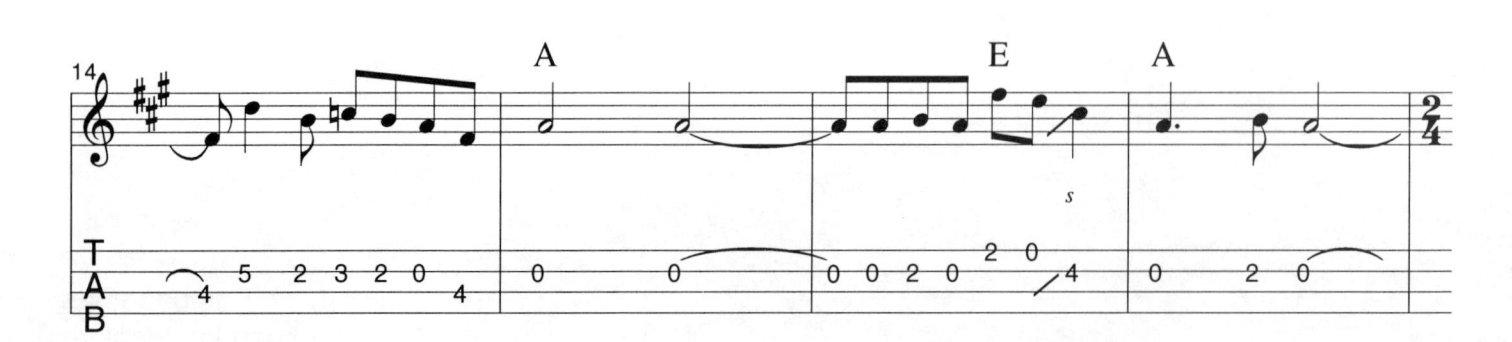

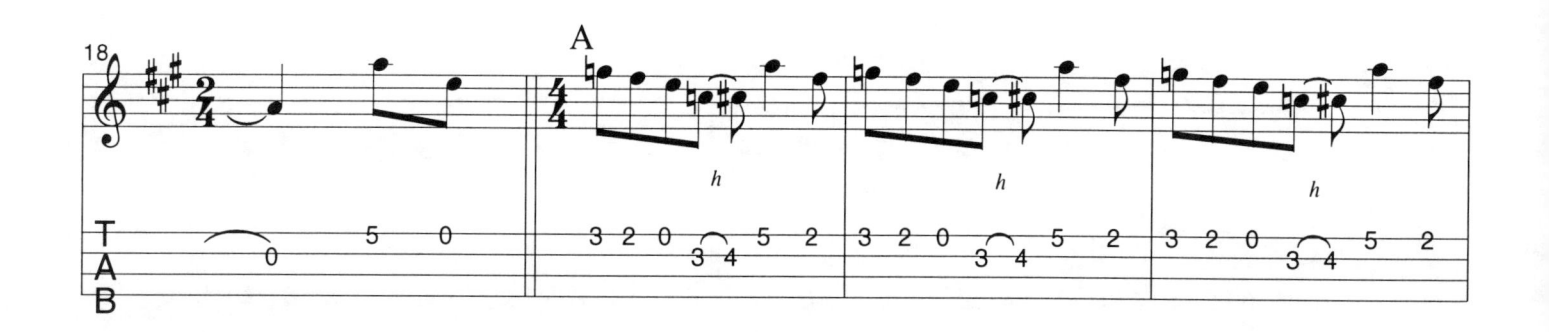

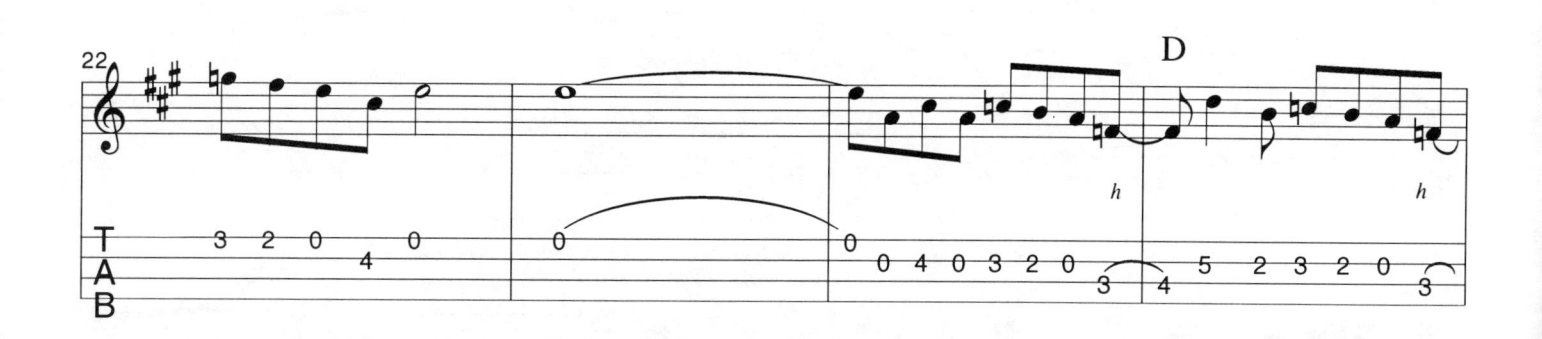

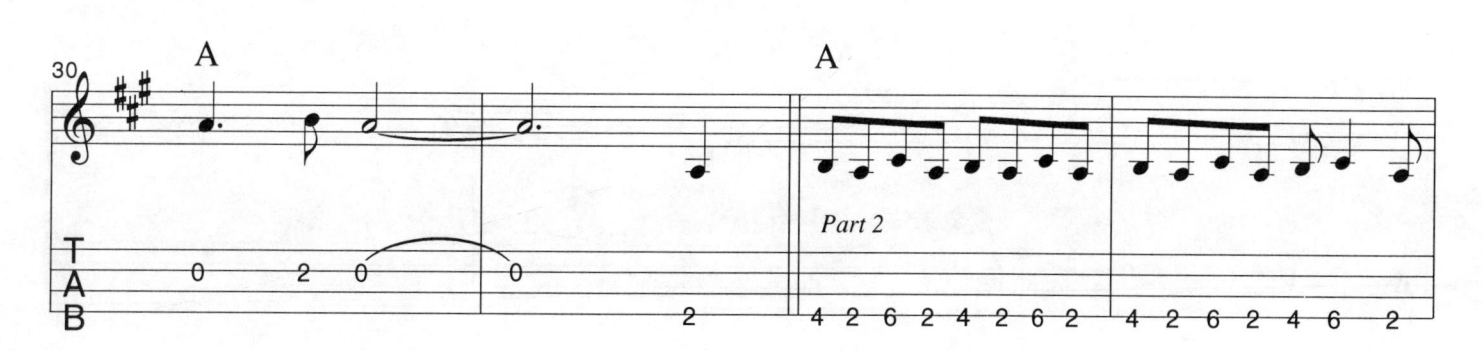

Carroll County Blues Mando 2

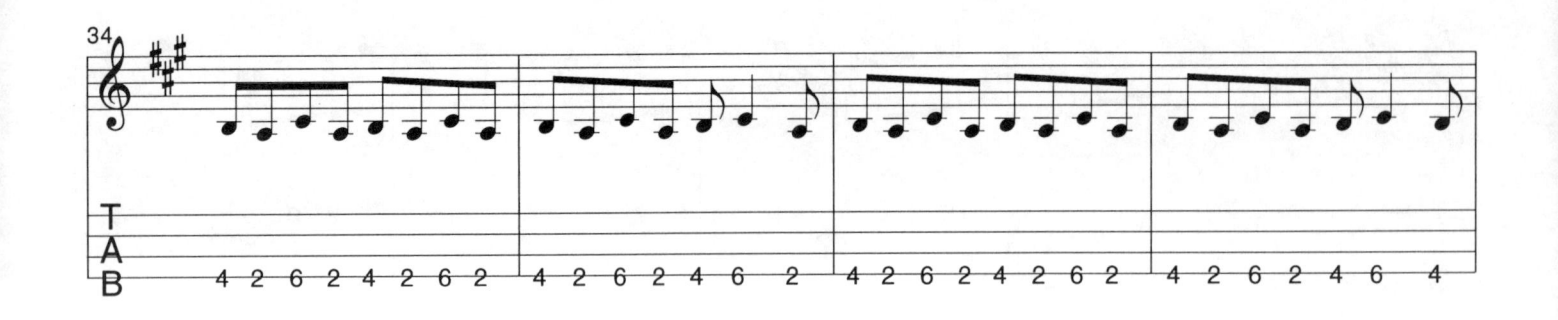

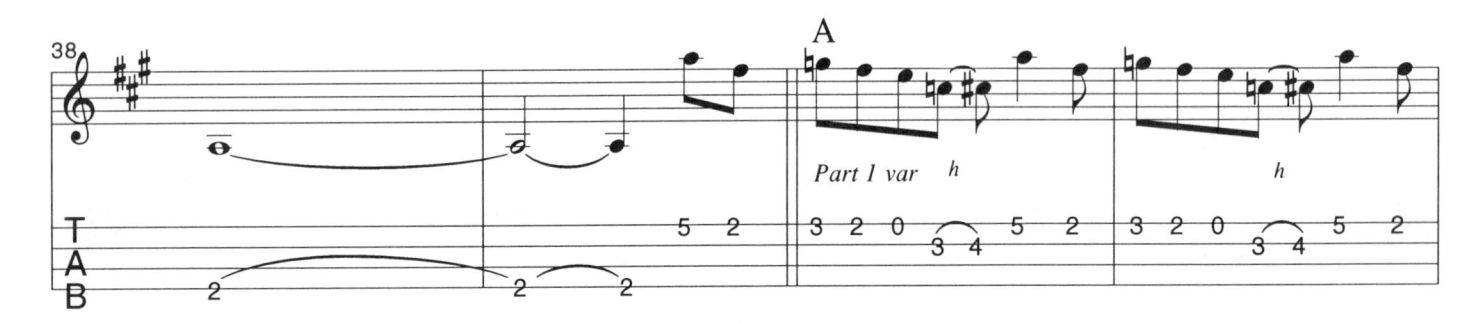

The second time this theme is played on the CD, the band adds two beats between measures 43 and 44.

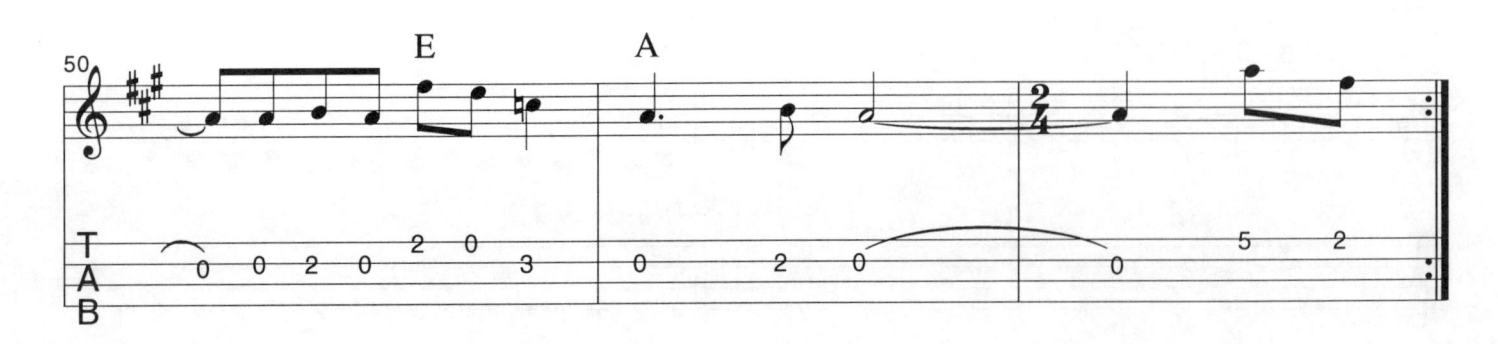

Carroll County Blues Mando 3

This page has been left blank to avoid awkward page turns

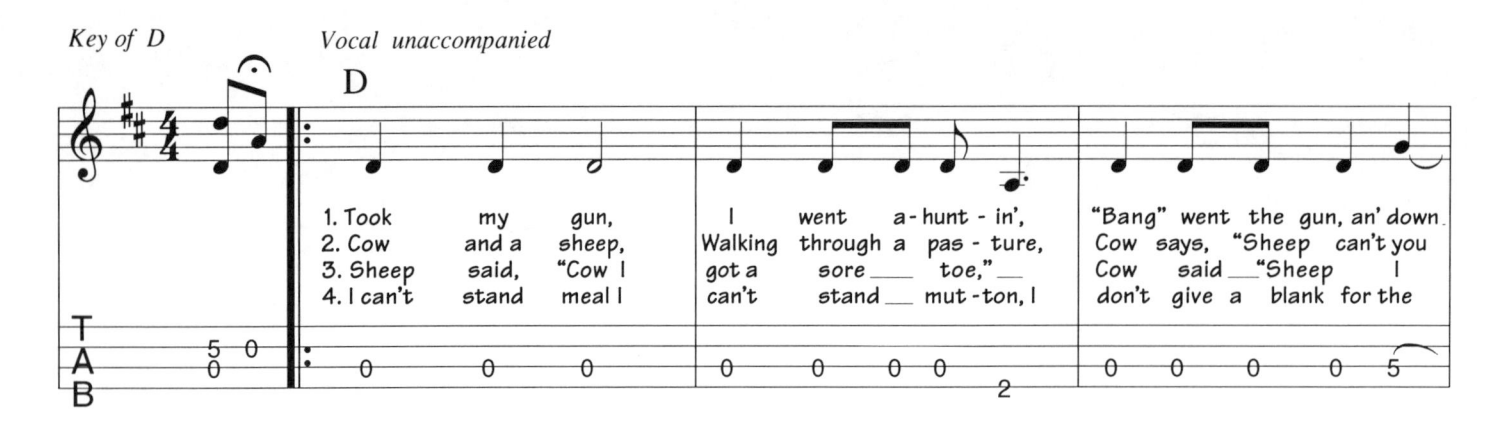

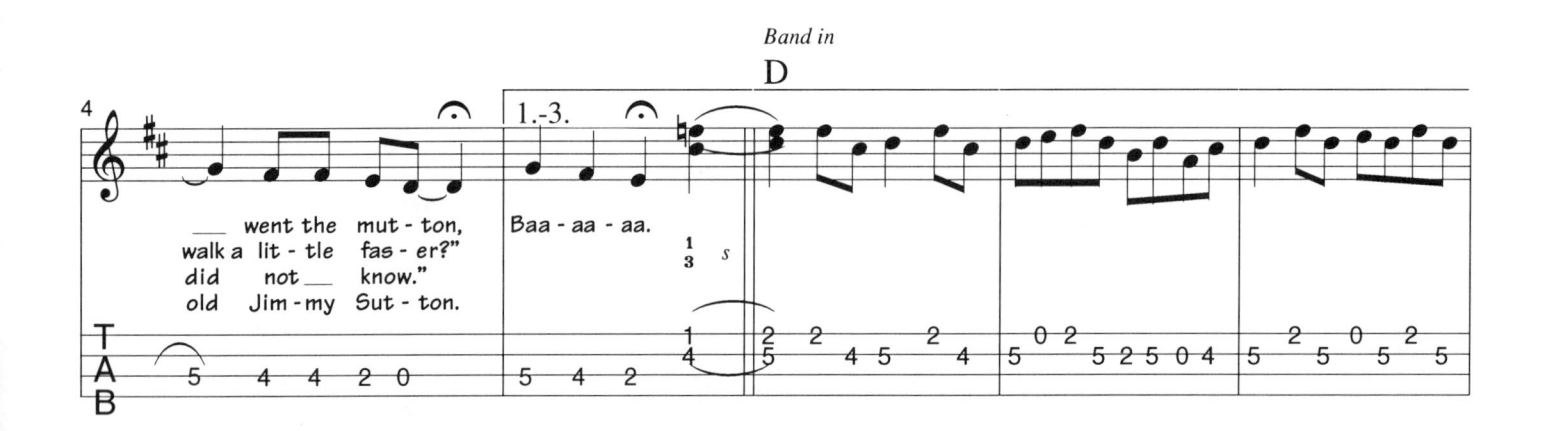

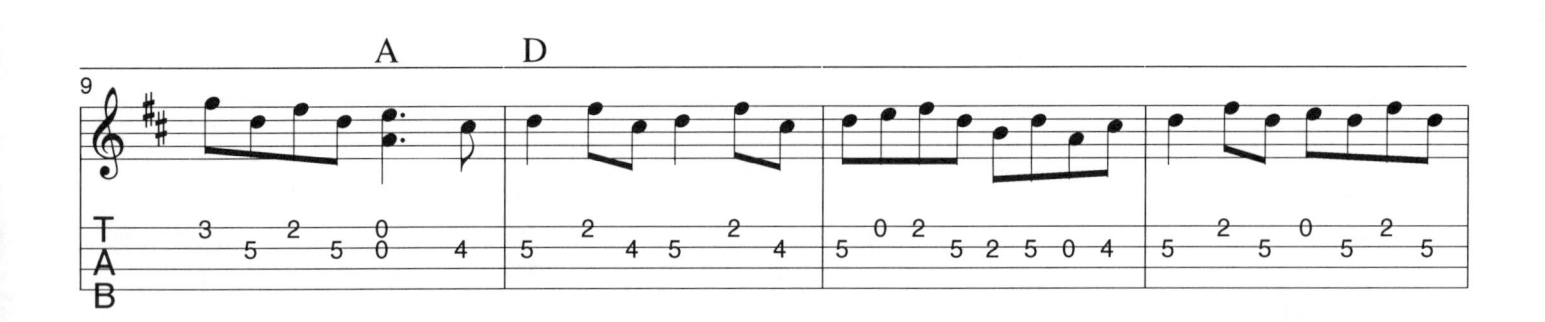

Old Jimmy Sutton

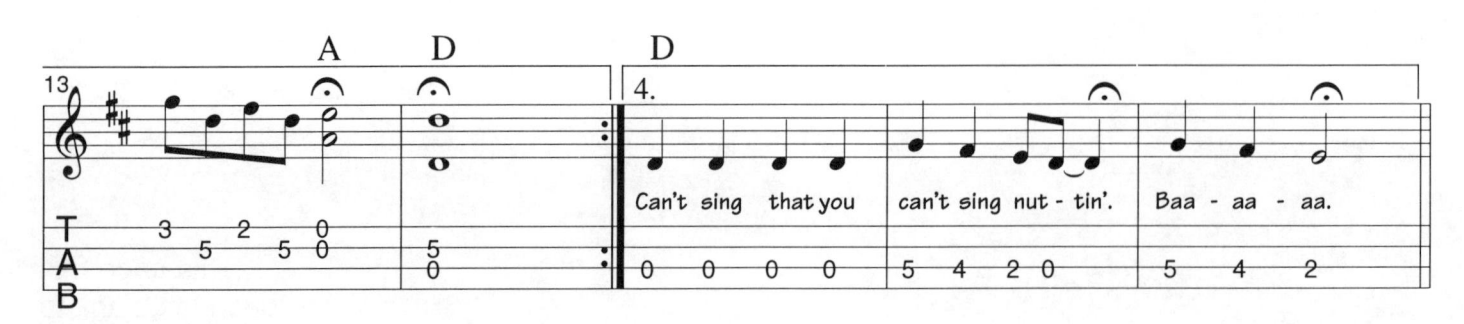

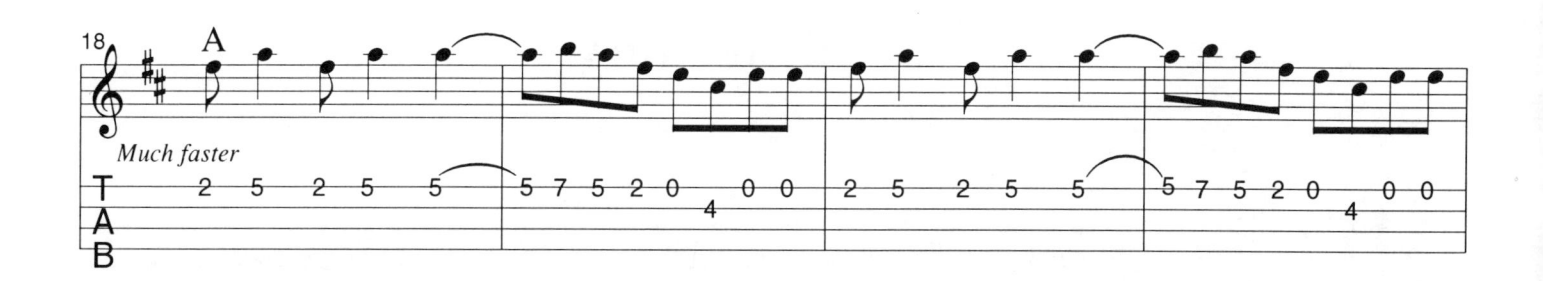

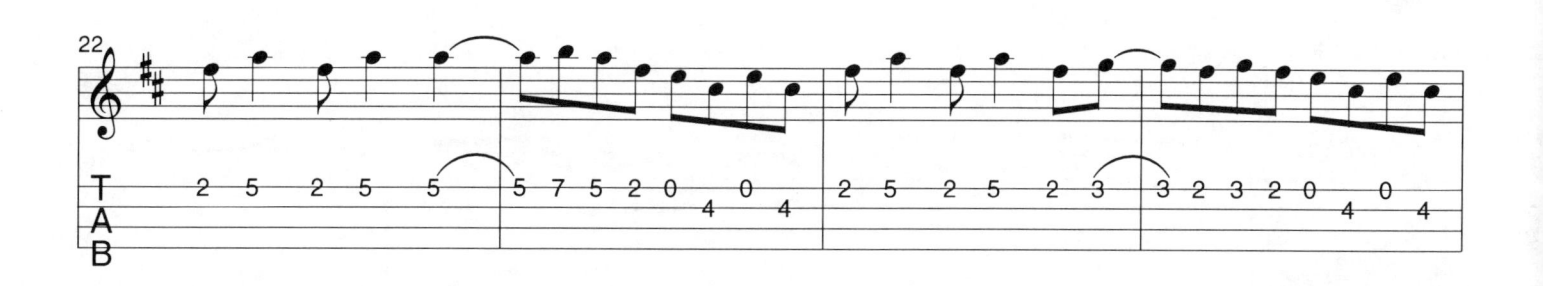

Old Jimmy Sutton Mando 2

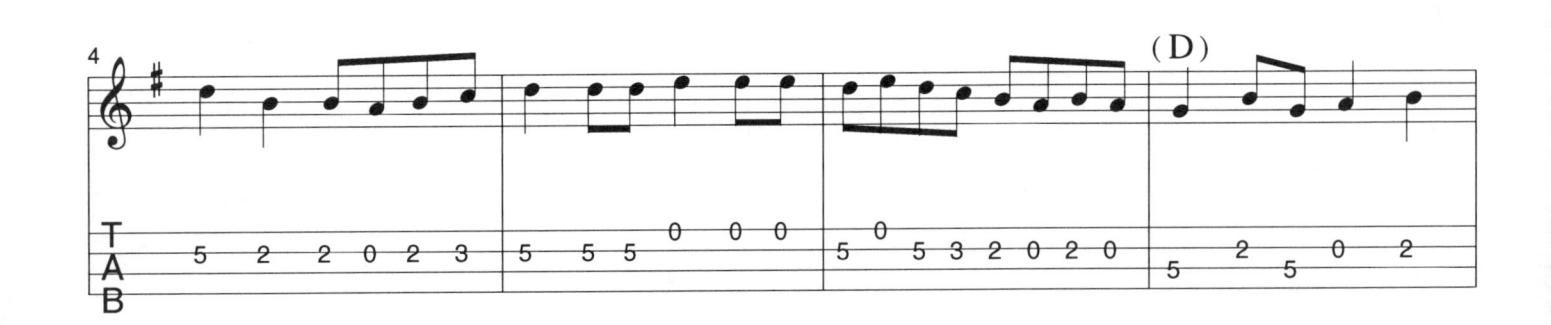

Devilish Mary

Key of G
Intro based on fiddle

Verse

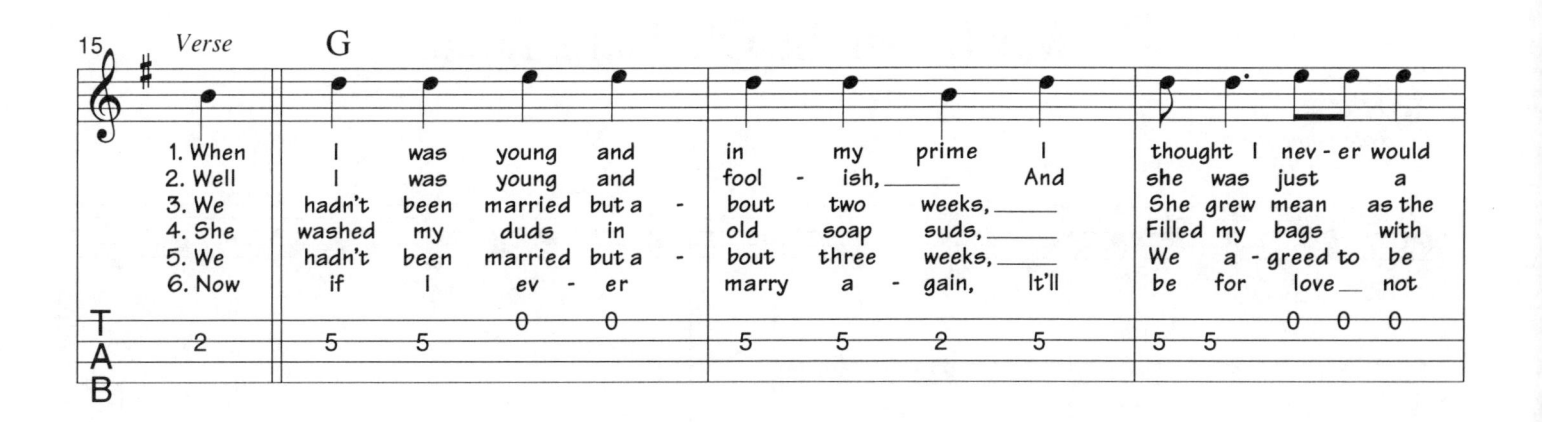

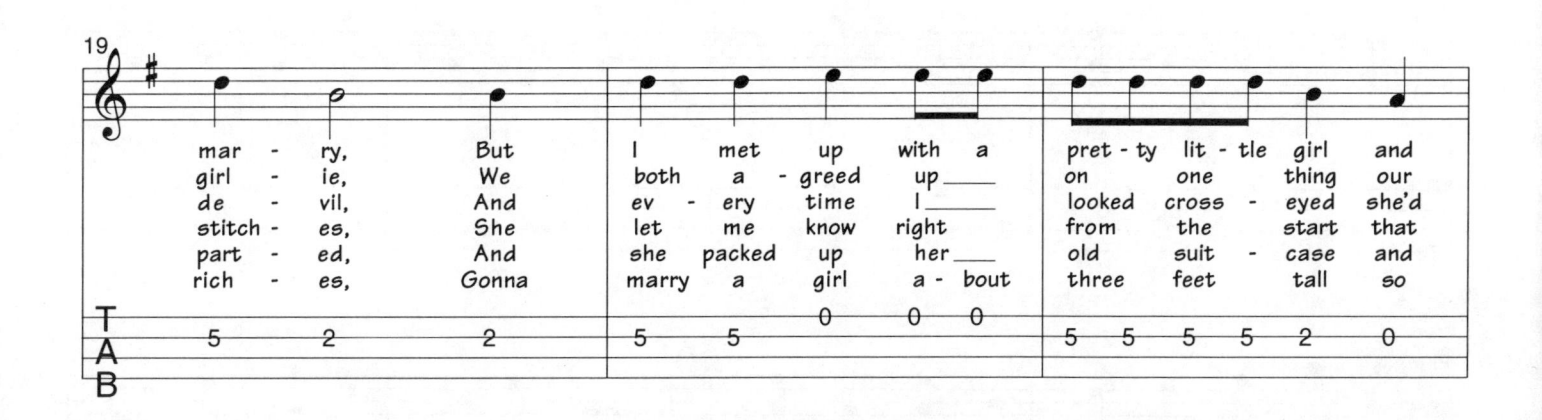

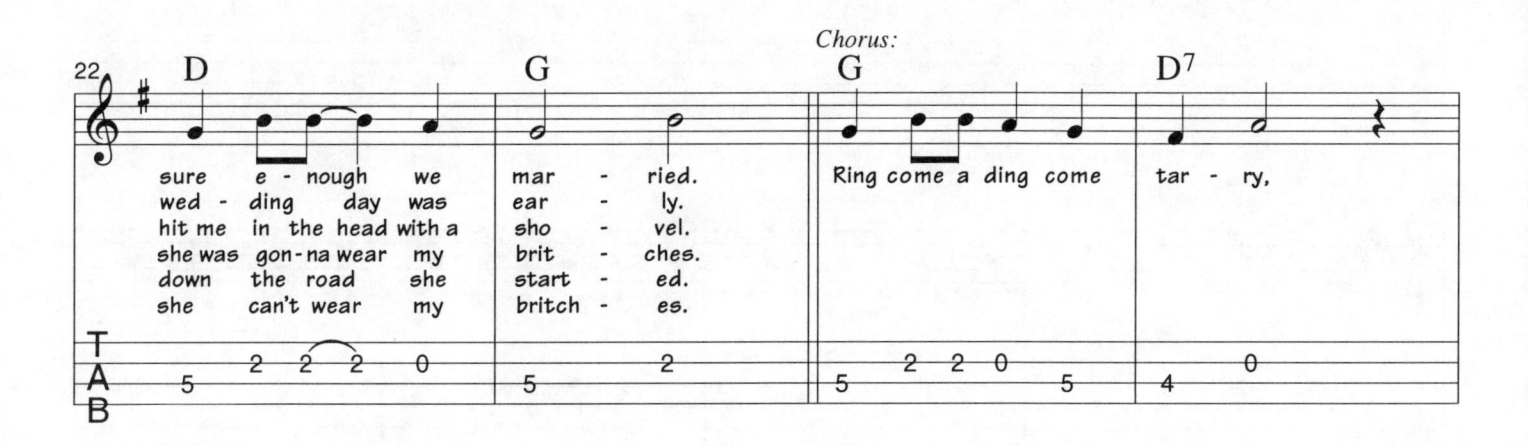

G

1. When I was young and in my prime I thought I never would marry, But I met up with a pretty little girl and sure enough we married.
2. Well I was young and foolish, And she was just a girlie, We both agreed up on one thing our wedding day was early.
3. We hadn't been married but about two weeks, She grew mean as the devil, And every time I looked cross-eyed she'd hit me in the head with a shovel.
4. She washed my duds in old soap suds, Filled my bags with stitches, She let me know right from the start that she was gonna wear my britches.
5. We hadn't been married but about three weeks, We agreed to be parted, And she packed up her old suitcase and down the road she started.
6. Now if I ever marry again, It'll be for love not riches, Gonna marry a girl about three feet tall so she can't wear my britches.

Chorus:

Ring come a ding come tarry, Prettiest girl ever I saw and her name was Devilish Mary.

Play M 1-14 between vocals

Devilish Mary Mando 2

Way Down the Old Plank Road

Key of D
Intro based on banjo

Fiddle intro
Vocal
1. I'd ra - ther be in Mem - phis with all the rain and hail,
2. I went down in Geor - gia to get on the gra - vy train, the
3. Oh Floss - ie, oh dear Floss - ie, What makes you treat me so? You
4. Eigh - teen pounds of meat a week and whis - key here to sell, Now
5. Mem - phis is a pret - ty town, Nash - ville is a beauty, If you
6. My wife died on Fri - day night, Satur - day she was buried,
Then to be in Geor - gia boys, tied to a ball and chain,
very next thing I heard a - bout, I was wear - ing a ball and chain,
caught me wearing a ball and chain and now my ank - le's sore,
how can a poor boy stay at home when the pretty girls look so well?
want to see them pret - ty girls now go to Chatt - a - noogie,
Sun - day was my court - ing day, Mon - day I got married,
Chorus
Won't get drunk no more, Won't get drunk no more, Won't get drunk no more way down the old plank road.

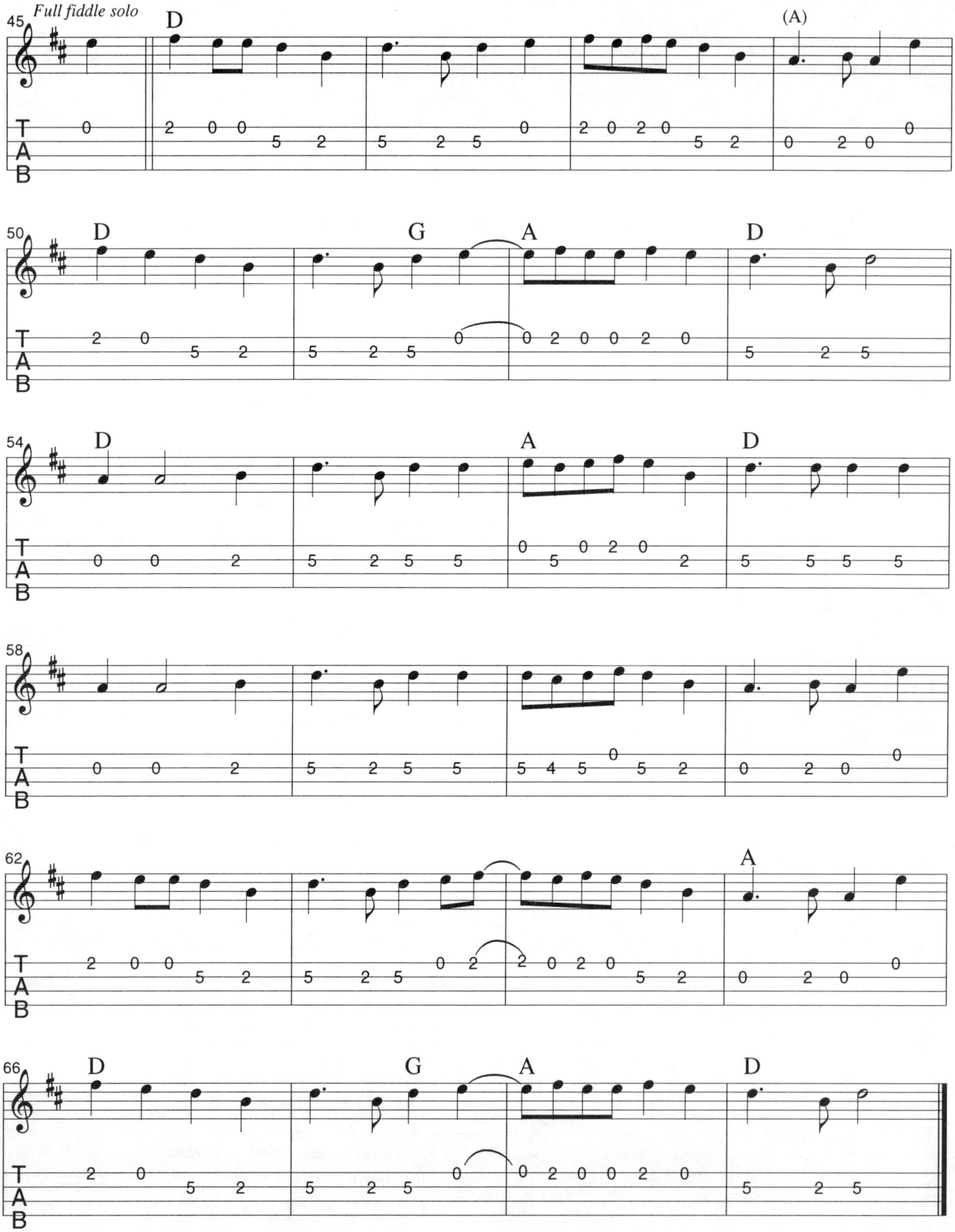
Full fiddle solo
D
(A)
D
G
A
D
D
A
D
A
D
G
A
D

Tater Patch

Key of D / A mixolydian

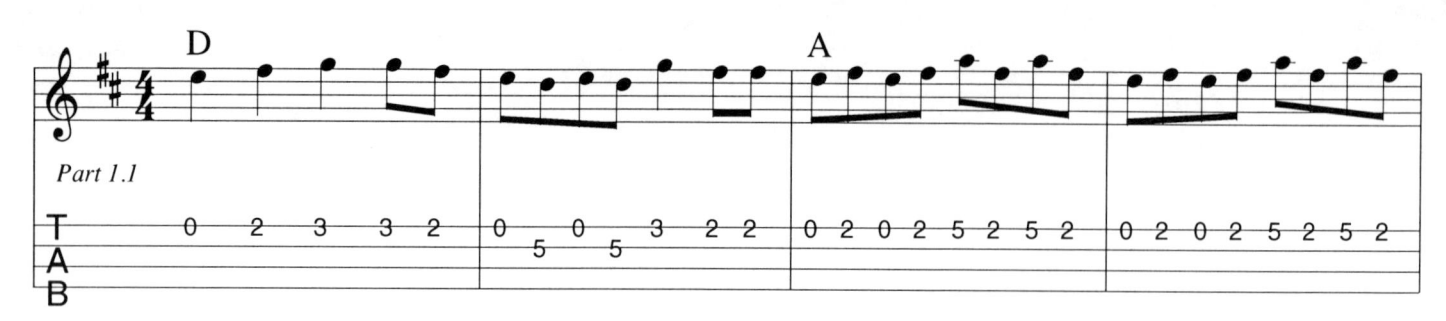

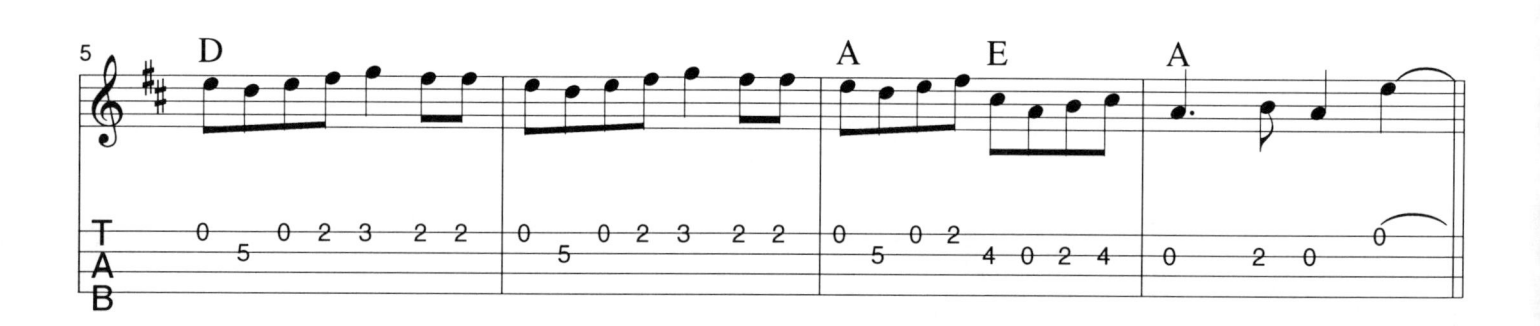

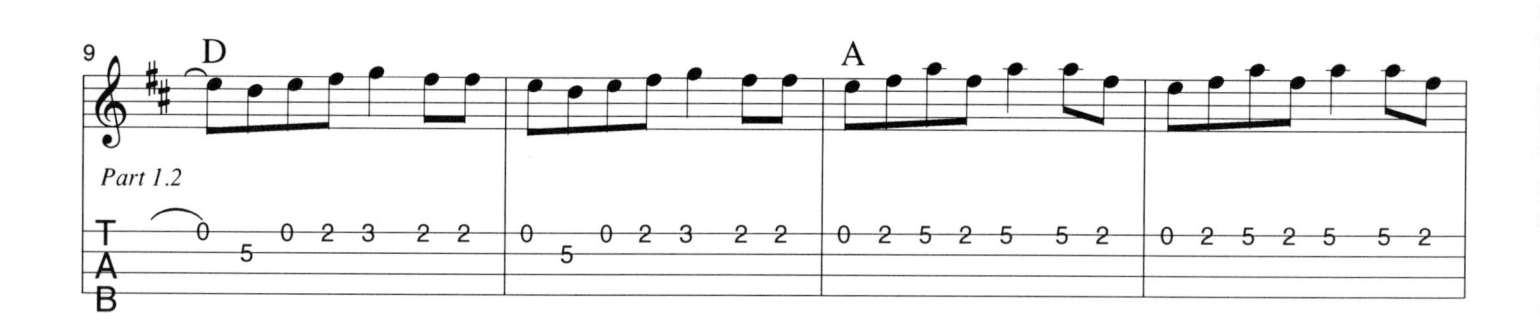

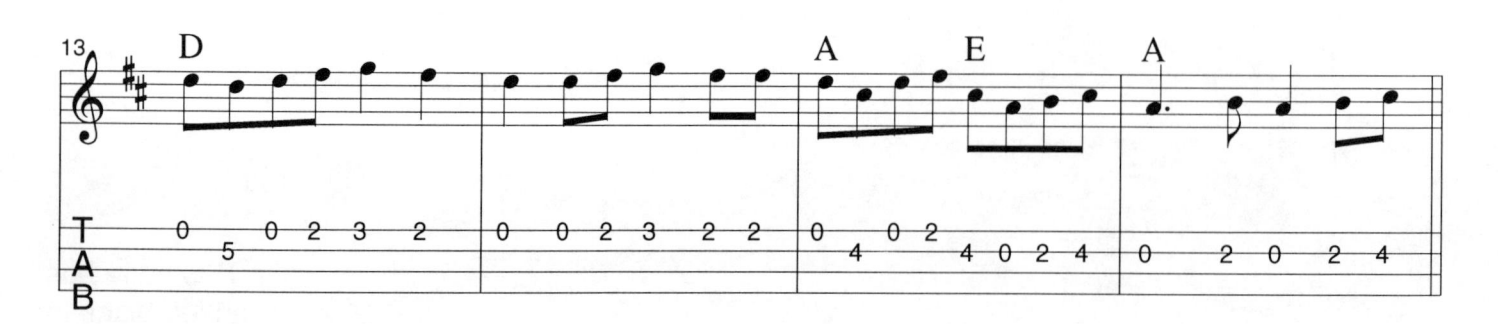

Tater Patch Mando 2

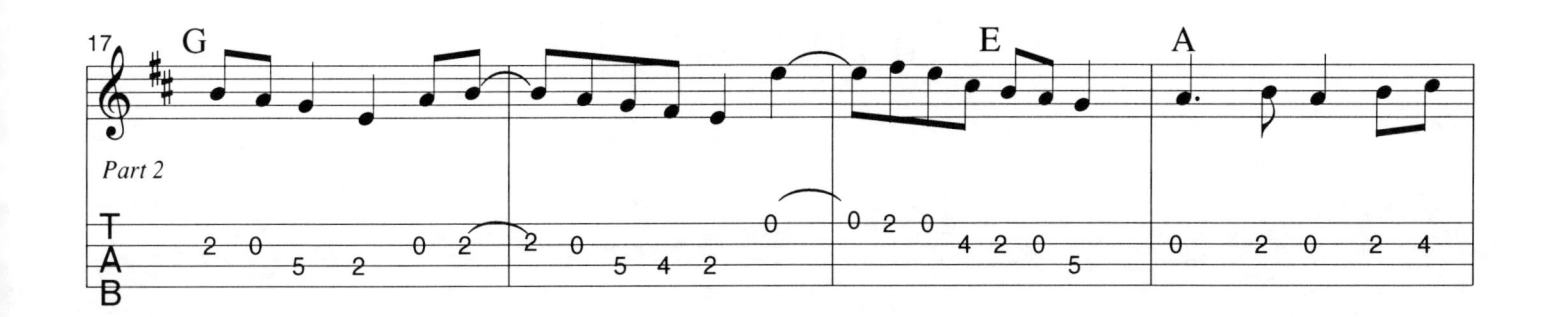

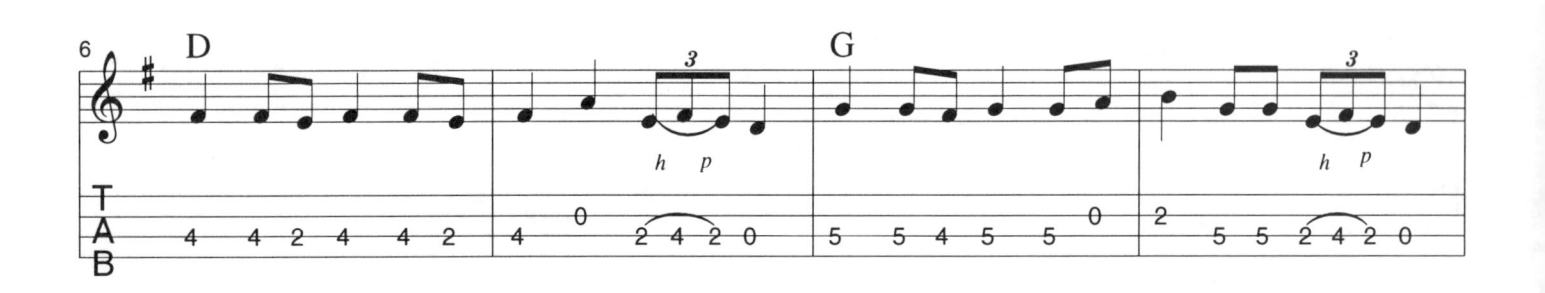

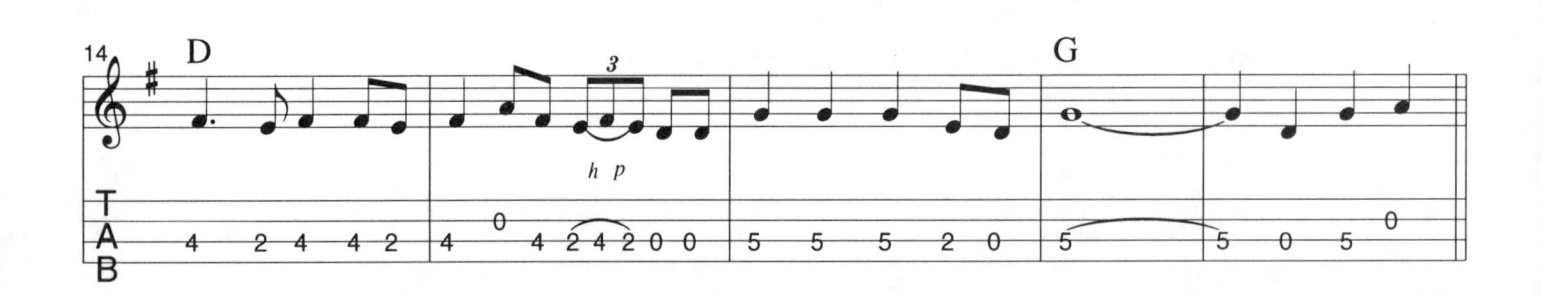

My Dixie Darling

23
D
G
27
31
D
35
G
G
Verse
1. Way down be- low the Mas - on Dix - on line,
2. I'm going down south gon - na have a big time,
39
D
There's where the hon-ey- suck-les are en - twined,
See my girl in old Caro - line, I'll
There's where the south - ern
drink my booze and

G
winds are blow - ing, There's where the dai - sies' grow - ing.
do as I please, For all those girls I long to squeeze,
All the girls of the North in their gay fin - e - ry, Twirl-ing a-round to a
Singing a song of Dix - ie Dar-ling There's where I
D
slow set - ee, Sing - ing a song of Dix - ie Dar - ling,
long to be go - ing, Down where the jelly roll's grow - ing,
p
G
Chorus
where I long to be. My Dix - ie
With my Dix - ie queen.
Dar - ling, Lis - ten to this song I sing,
D
G
Be- neath the sil - ver moon, With the ban - jo right in

tune. My heart is ev - er true, I love no one but
you, My Dix - ie Dar - ling, My Dix - ie queen.
D
G
Solo based on guitar
G
D
G
D
G

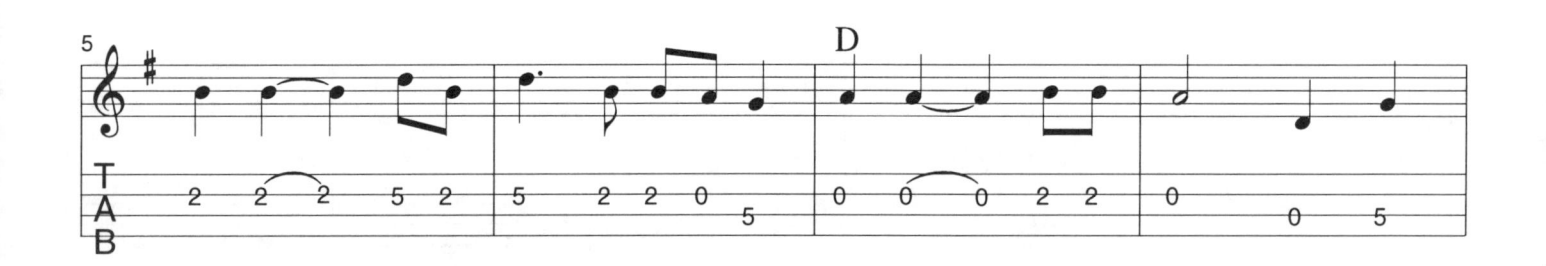

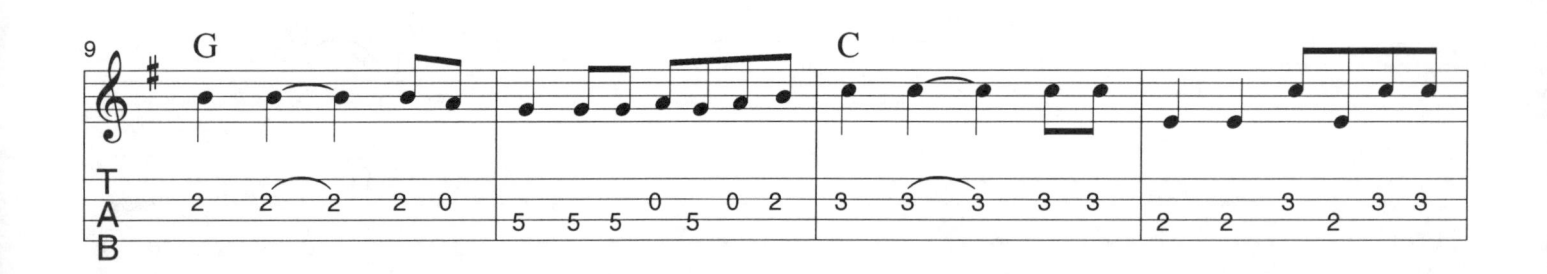

Free Little Bird

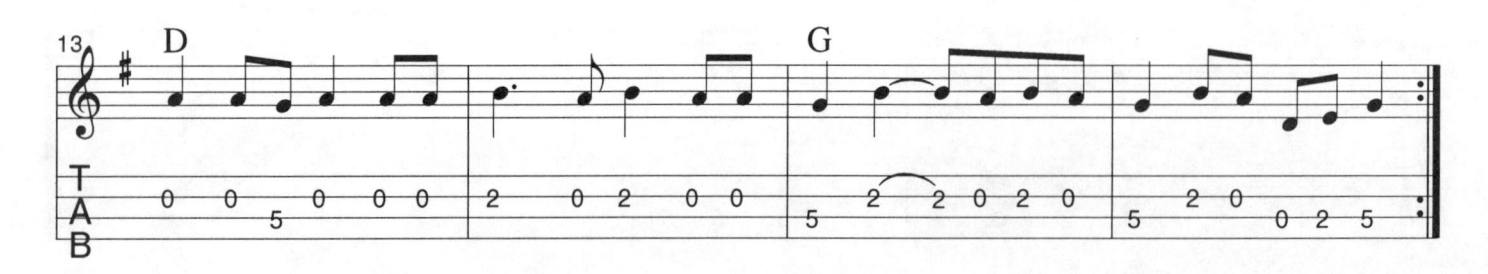

Key of G
Intro based on fiddle

Chorus
Verses
I'm as free a lit - tle bird as I can be, I can be, I'm as free a lit - tle bird as I can be,
1. I'll never build my nest on the ground, On the ground, I'll nev - er build my nest on the ground, I'll
2. I'll never steal the hon - ey from the tree, From the tree, I'll nev - er steal the hon - ey from the tree, I'll
3. 'Bout as fit a fish as I can be, I would-n't bite a hook or a line, I'd
build my nest in a white oak tree, Where the bad boys they can-not both - er me.
build my nest in a weeping willow tree, Where the bad boys they can-not tear me down.
steal a kiss from my sweet darling's lips, And steal her a - way a - cross the sea.
swim way out to the middle of the sea, And leave all them big fish be - hind.
G
D
C
TAB
h
Repeat chorus after each verse.

Been All Around This World

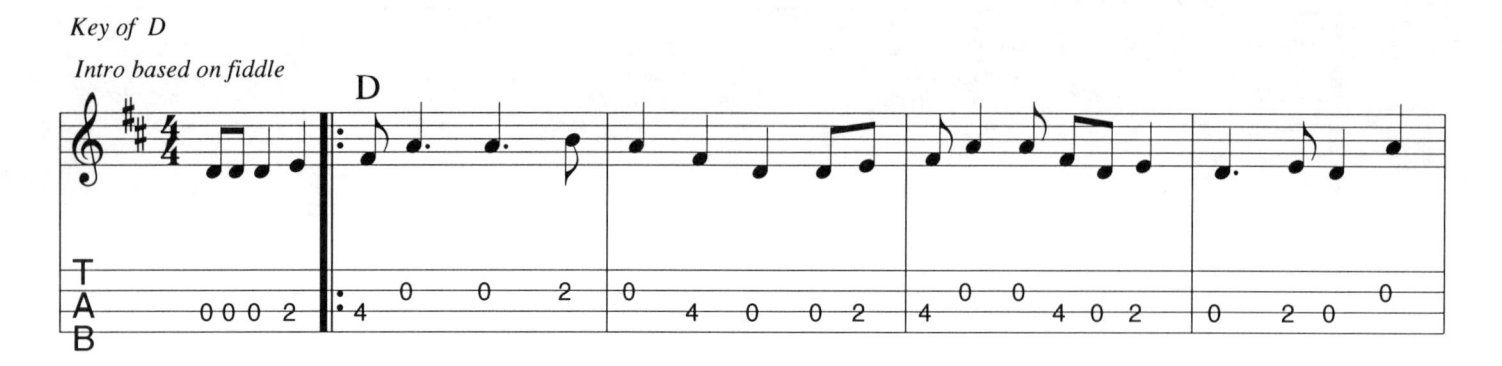

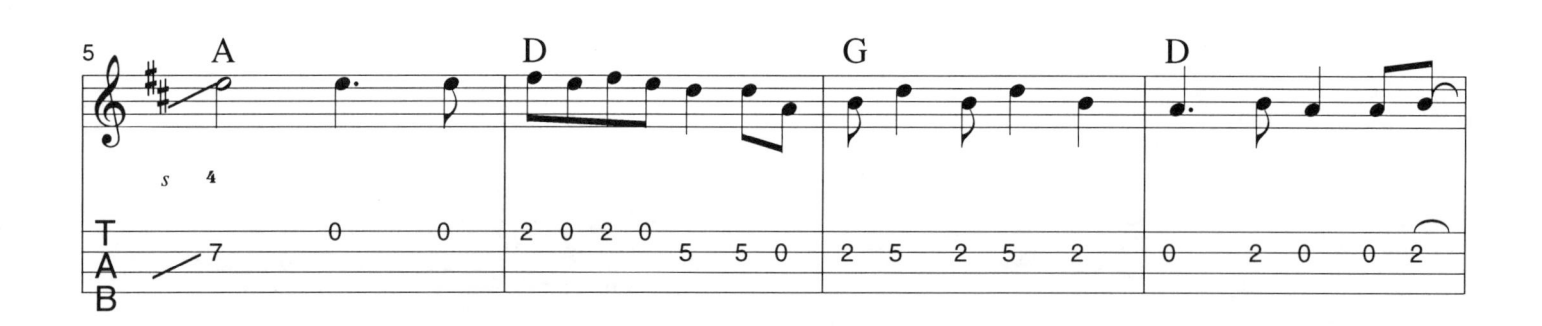

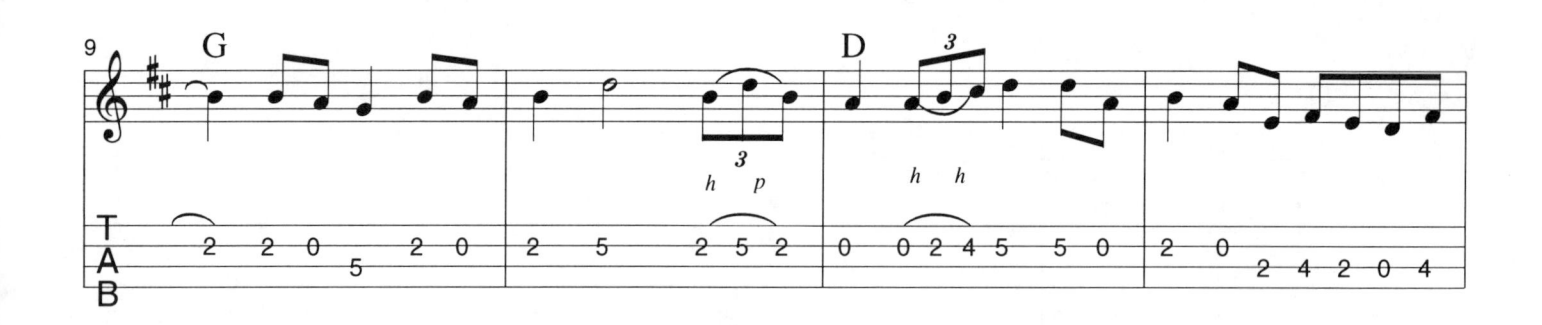

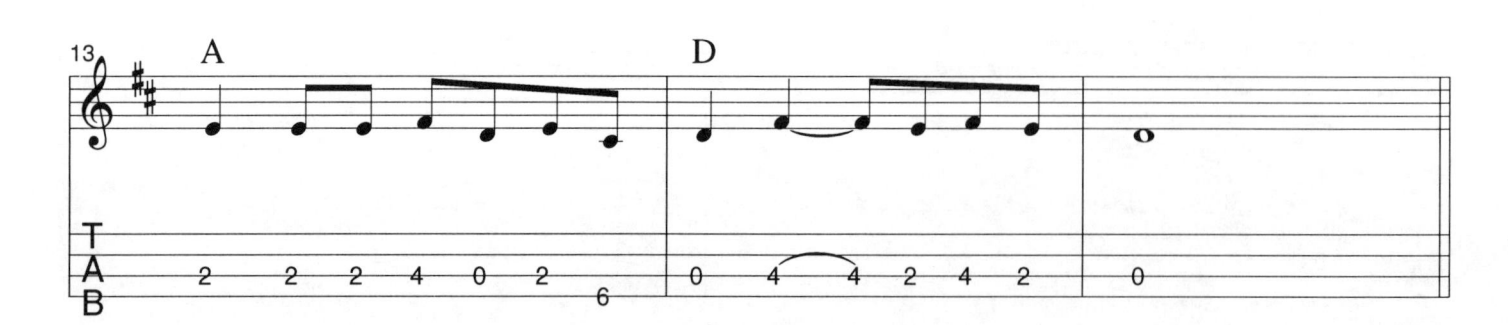

Verse
D
Verse order: 1, 2, 3, 1, 4, 5, 3, 1
1. Hang me, oh hang me, I'll be dead and gone,
2. Lu - lu, oh Lu - lu, Come and o - pen up that door,
3. Going up on the moun - tain, There I'll take my stand,
4. Ma - ma and Pa - pa, and little sister make three,
5. Working on that new rail - road with mud up to my knees,
A
D
Hang me, oh hang me and I'll be dead and gone,
Lu - lu, oh Lu Lu come and o - pen up that door,
Going up on the moun tain, There I'll take my stand,
Ma - ma and Pa pa and little sis - ter make three, You
Working on that new rail - road with the mud up to my knees,
G
D
G
Not the hang - ing that I mind it's lay - ing in the jail so long, Lord, Lord I
Before I have to o - pen it with my old for - ty four,
Pis - tol in my pock - et and a rif le in my hand,
know they've come to see me hang - ing from the gal - lows tree,
Working for big John Hen - ry you know he's so hard to please,
A
D
been all a - round this world.
p
h

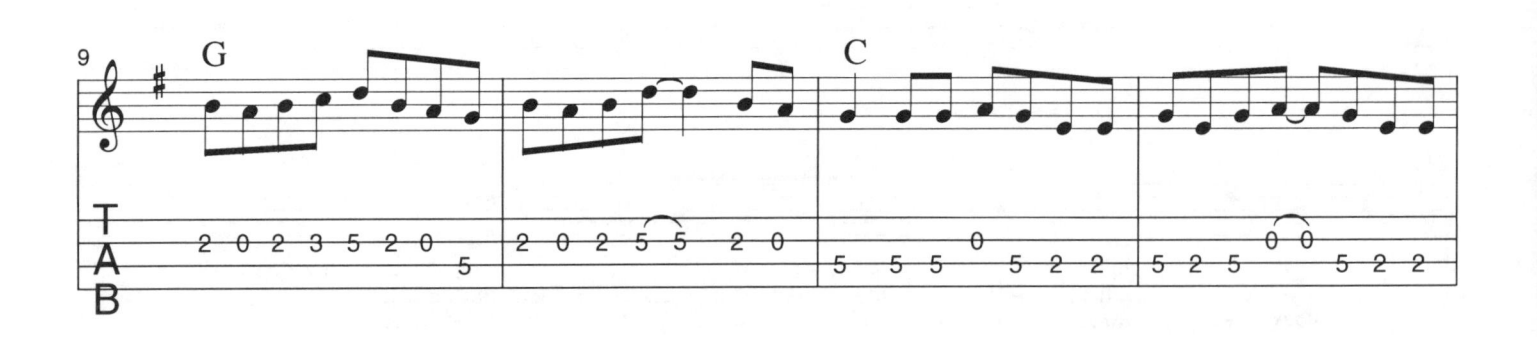

Goodbye Miss Liza Jane

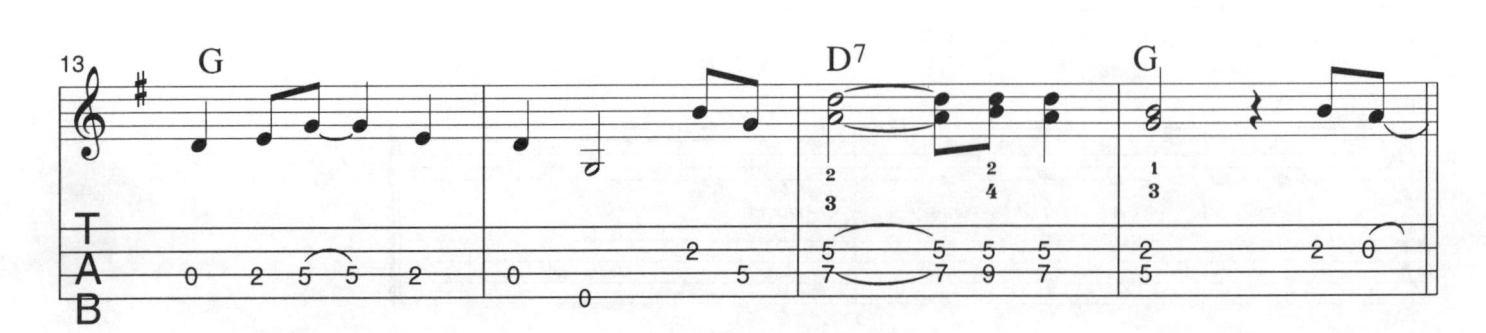

Key of G
Ensemble intro & solo:

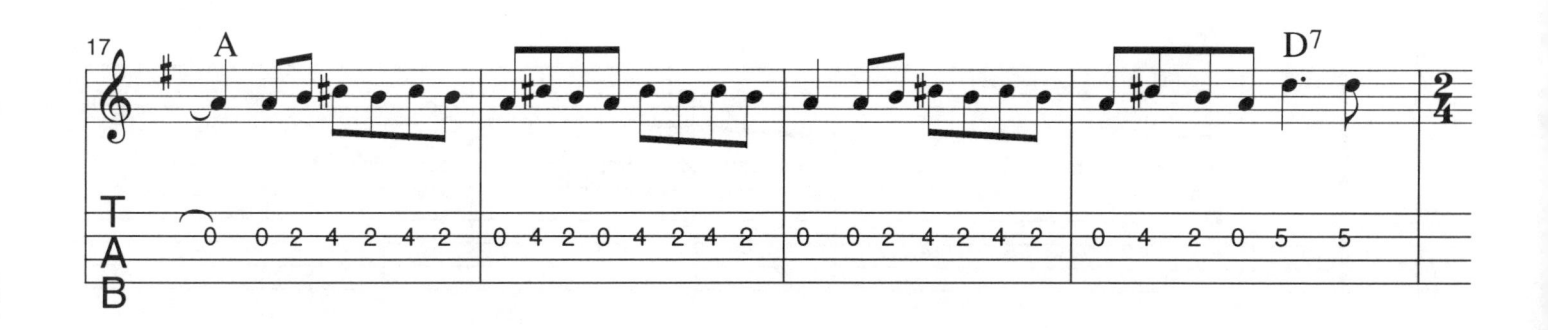

Goodbye Miss Liza 2

Verse
G C
1. Oh look-a here Li-za lis-ten to me, You ain't the girl that you
2. Gim-me a back my gold watch and chain, Gim-me the umbrella 'cause
G
pro-mised to be, Did-n't you say you'd al-ways be true-hoo-
it might rain, Gim-me the clothes that I paid for too,
D7 G
hoo? Saw you out rid-in' with Mis-ter Brown,
Dive in the trunk now gim-me those things,
C G
Now I'm the laugh-in' stock of the town, Peo-ple said to
Gimme a-back my di-a-mond ring, Get Mister Brown to
D7 G
nev-er trust you hoo.
dress you all up new.
TAB

Chorus:
A
Throw up your hands babe I'm gon - na go, I was a good man when I had the
0 0 0 4 4 0 0 0 0 4 0 0 0 4 0 0 0 0 0
D7 G C
dough. So it's good - bye Miss Li - za, I'm going to
5 5 5 0 0 2 5 2 0 0 5
D7 G
leave you, You know when I go, I'm the fel - low with the
2 5 4 5 4 4 5 5 4 5 5 4 5 0
C
dough. So sing a lit - tle song, tra-vel a - long, yes tra-vel a - long,
2 2 3 3 3 3 2 3 3 3 2 2 2 3 3 3 2 2
G D7 G
Bid me good day ba - by I'm on my way, Good - bye Miss Li - za Jane.
5 5 5 3 3 3 2 2 2 0 5 5 5 2 0 5

Lee Highway Blues

Key of D

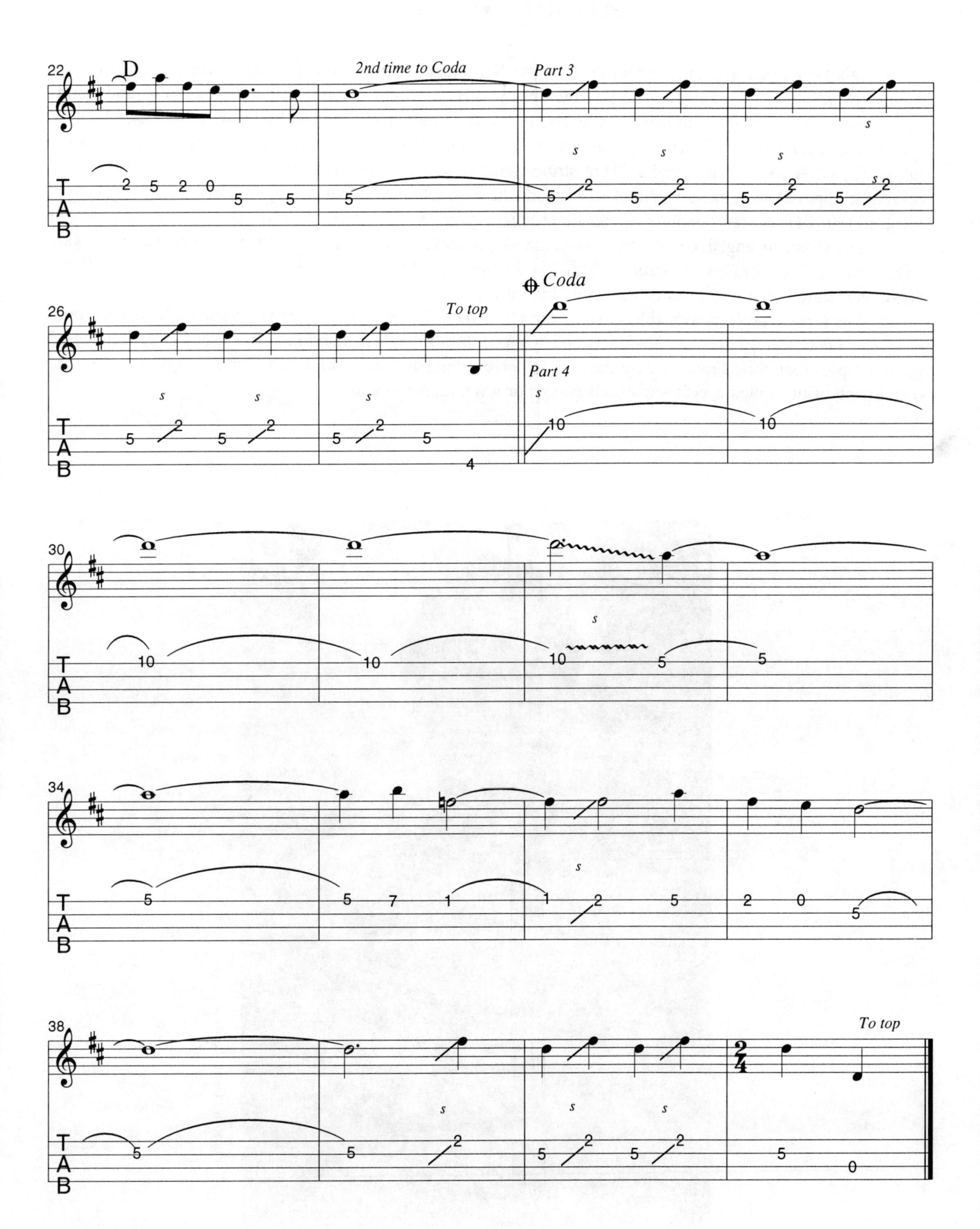

Lee Highway Blues Mando 2

About Dix Bruce

Dix Bruce is a musician and writer from the San Francisco Bay Area. He has authored over forty books, recordings, and videos for Mel Bay Publications. He does studio work on guitar, mandolin, and banjo and has recorded two LPs with mandolin legend Frank Wakefield, eight big band CDs with the Royal Society Jazz Orchestra, his own collection of American folk songs entitled "My Folk Heart" on which he plays guitar, mandolin, autoharp and sings, and a CD of string swing & jazz entitled "Tuxedo Blues." He contributed two original compositions to the soundtrack of Harrod Blank's acclaimed documentary "Wild Wheels." He has released four CDs of traditional American songs and originals with guitarist Jim Nunally.

Dix Bruce arranged, composed, played mandolin, and recorded music for the CD ROM computer game "The Sims" for the Maxis Corporation. "Sims" is the newest entry in the best selling "Sim City" series. His music is featured on a virtual radio station within the game.

The newest projects available to you from Dix Bruce & Mel Bay are: "First Lessons: Mandolin" (book & CD, or DVD set) for absolute beginners and "Getting Into Bluegrass mandolin" (book & CD set). It doesn't get any easier than this! From holding the pick to performing easy mandolin tunes. For a complete and up-to-date listing of titles please visit www.melbay.com or www.musixnow.com.

Photo by Gene Tortora

Also by Dix Bruce:

CDs, videos, and instructional books by Dix Bruce: (For songlists and full details, contact Musix, PO Box 231007, Pleasant Hill, CA 94523. E-mail: info@musixnow.com).

Doc Watson & Clarence Ashley 1960-62 for Guitar (book & CD sets of transcriptions: chords, melodies, lyrics, Doc's solos & rhythm playing, incredible repertoire).

You Can Teach Yourself Country Guitar (Mel Bay).

Guide to the Capo, Transposing, and the Nashville Numbering System (Mel Bay). A thorough and thoughtful explanation of music theory, using the capo, and how the Nashville Numbering System works.

BackUp Trax: Old Time Fiddle Tunes Vol. I (Mel Bay). Jam all night long with the band on old time and fiddle tunes. You play all the leads and the band never gets tired!

BackUp Trax: Basic Blues for Guitar (Mel Bay). Jam all night long with the newest set of hot blues grooves: Delta, Country, Urban, Modern, it's all here!

You Can Teach Yourself Mandolin (Mel Bay).

Famous Mandolin Pickin' Tunes book and CD set from the QwikGuide series.

From Fathers to Sons CD by Dix Bruce & Jim Nunally of folk, bluegrass, & hot guitar picking (Musix CD/C 104).

The Way Things Are CD by Dix Bruce & Jim Nunally. More hot picking & great new songs by the duo. (Musix CD/C 105).

My Folk Heart CD by Dix Bruce, solo & small group, traditional American folk music (Musix CD/C101). With Jim Nunally, Tom Rozum, and John Reischman.

Tuxedo Blues CD by Dix Bruce, string swing & jazz (Musix CD/C102). With Bob Alekno on mandolin, David Balakrishnan on violin, Mike Wollenberg on bass.

In My Beautiful Dream CD by Dix Bruce & Jim Nunally. Mostly original songs plus lots of hot guitar picking. (Musix CD 106).

Brothers at Heart CD by Dix Bruce & Jim Nunally. Brother duet style singing on classic and new songs in the traditional style.